C000017061

THE SUMMER I FELL FOR MY BEST FRIEND

LEGACY INN

SARA JANE WOODLEY

Cover Photography by
KAMIL MACNIAK

ELEVENTH AVENUE PUBLISHING

A THANK YOU TO MY READERS

In August 2020, I released my first book in the Legacy Inn series. I was passionate about this project, and I was hopeful that people would like my stories as much as I loved writing them. But, I never could have imagined that I would be blessed with the most amazing community of readers!

I can't begin to tell you how thankful I am for each and every one of you. I've loved every message, email, and review, and always appreciate hearing from you. Your support and kind words have been some of the *best* parts of this journey.

To my Advance Reader Team, thank you for your incredibly valuable and consistent feedback. It means so much to me to have such a wonderful group of dedicated readers.

Love always,

Sara Jane

1

BREE

I park my Ford Escape just inside the gates, grazing my mom's prize hydrangeas. My mom yells at me when I park this close; she tells me that my cheap SUV will destroy her flowers. I park there anyway, just to see her sweat a little.

The portable radio blasts static — soothing white noise — before I turn it off and kill the ignition. The world is silent and I look at the dark windows of our house.

Tonight's storm was mediocre. The storm was moving fast over the prairies about an hour from Edendale High, turning the sky to bruised shades of blue and purple. While others took cover inside, I drove into the darkness, headed straight for the whirl of angry clouds.

The wind howled and ripped leaves from tree branches. Rain fell in torrential sheets as the sky turned black. Parked on the side of a gravel road, Garth — my SUV — rocked on its tires. My adrenaline pumped the way it always does when I chase storms. I chewed a fruit roll-up and waited for the first strike of lightning.

Then, the weather shifted. The sky went from an angry

black to a dull grey, the storm merely a whisper of what I'd hoped for. I sighed, turned on my thriller audiobook, and peeled out. The storm in the prairies was disappointing, but another storm awaited me at home.

This particular storm had been building all year, courtesy of my strategy and hard work.

The noise of the lock echoes as I shut the door behind me. The house is silent, but there's no point in trying to be quiet. There's a single light on in the family room, and I know what awaits me at the end of the long, dark stretch of hallway.

Wanting to build up to the fireworks, I take my time, stopping to straighten one of our family photos. In the photo, we all look so happy. Posed. Fake. Me and my sister, Isla, are grasping hands as we stand in front of my parents.

Right after the photo was taken, my parents broke into an argument. To distract Isla, I poked her in the side and got her to chase me. Those stupid hay bales... I tripped over one and went down screaming. Isla landed on top of me and we fought in the hay until we couldn't breathe from laughing. My mom's face was a brilliant shade of burgundy as she pulled us up and glared daggers at me.

Here we go.

I take a breath and saunter into the family room.

My mom is sitting straight-backed on the sofa like a British royal. My dad is next to her, head tilted to the side. Probably sleeping.

"So." My voice is breezy. "Who had a good day?"

I flop onto a chair and open my pre-packaged sandwich. A loaded silence echoes from the sofa... the calm before the storm.

"I had a great day," I say, speaking with my mouth full. "The seniors pulled a prank on the teachers for the last day.

You'd be amazed what you can do with a dozen fake spiders, three socks, and—"

"This is funny to you, Aubrey?" Mom's voice is low, the rumbling of distant thunder.

"Dearest Kate, to what are you referring?" I look at her innocently. She hates it when I use her name.

She stands, holding my report card in her hand. My dad is slumped over and she shakes his shoulder. "Lionel. Wake up and discipline your daughter!"

A snort and my dad's eyes pop open. His glasses hang off one ear and his hair stands on end. "You know exactly what you did, young lady."

The classic Lionel answer. I refrain from rolling my eyes.

My mom frowns so deeply I think her botox might fail. A thrill runs through me. She's going to snap, which means we might have an open, honest conversation. My mom only thinks about me when she's angry. Or does she get angry when she thinks about me? Chicken or egg, I guess.

My mom shakes the report card in front of her. "Did you think that we wouldn't find out about this?"

"Paper? Oh, Kate, paper's been around for ages. There's printer paper, recycled paper, toilet paper, tissue..."

My mom laughs wickedly. "So clever, aren't you? Always so clever... But if you're so clever, how did you end up failing English?"

Whoa. Failed? I didn't know I failed English. I was angling to get a solid C.

I need to choose my words carefully. Arguing with Mom is like defusing a bomb — cut the wrong wire and everything explodes. "I did well in my classes, overall."

"Like that matters." She glares. "Did you even go to school this year or were you spending all your time on your lightning hunts?"

"Storm chasing."

Mom's face twitches. "Oh, so now you care about English?"

A lump forms in my throat. I tend to tapdance along the line of what's considered acceptable, but it seems I've gone too far to one side. Time to put it in reverse. "I'm sorry."

"You're not a good enough liar to get away with that." Mom's voice is surprisingly calm. "Did you really think you could pull a stunt like this and come on the family vacation to Europe?"

My stomach drops like I'm in an elevator and the cord's been cut. I carefully compose my face into a mask of calm indifference. "What are you saying?"

"Your actions over the year have been unacceptable," my mom says. "Talking back to your dad and I, skipping out on important events, and denting your car with your foolish storm stunts. These grades are the final straw. English was the one course you needed, Aubrey. The one course we expected of you—"

My heart pounds, blood rushing in my ears so I can't hear my mom go on about what she expects from me and my future. I'll be attending an Ivy League business school immediately upon my graduation from Edendale High. To get in, I'll need to top grades in everything. Especially English. This year, I figured I could skip most English classes to go storm chasing, as long as I did well enough on the final exam.

I knew they'd be mad. But I didn't think they'd take my summer away from me.

"Your dad and I have decided that you will not be coming to Europe this summer. Instead, you'll be working at Legacy Inn. Maybe Delia can teach you some responsibility, seeing as you won't listen to us." My mom gathers my report card. "You'll also be retaking English next year. And you will get an A."

My throat is dry and my vision is blurred. The world spins. "You're leaving me here. Alone."

"Your irresponsibility, your carelessness, your deliberate disregard for anyone that's not you hurts everyone. There are consequences to your actions, Aubrey. If you want to blame someone, blame yourself."

There's a number of gestures or words I'd love to use in reply, but a sob rushes to my throat. There's no way I'm going to let them see me cry.

"Your loss." I force the words from my mouth and calmly exit the room. Once I hit the hallway, I break into a run and go to my bedroom. My eyes sting, but the bedroom door is closed before I break into uncontrollable tears.

2

BREE

*M*y face is wet with tears, my breath coming in short gasps.

A soft knock on my door interrupts my despair.

"Bree? Can I come in? Please?"

My sister. I have to be strong for her. I wipe the tears from my face, compose myself, and open the door. Downstairs, I can hear the raised voices — my mom's blaring tone, and then a quick word from my dad.

"What's up, kiddo?"

"They're fighting. Again."

Isla rolls her blue eyes and splays herself across the bed. She's wearing the pajama shirt and shorts I bought her to match my own. The cartoon bee on the shirt shouts to "Bee Kind," a gentler message than the angry words downstairs. They're arguing about me, most likely. Though it could just as easily be about the breadbox not being shut properly.

"What was the story tonight?" Isla flips open my computer screen.

"Make yourself at home, why don't you?" I laugh as she enters my password. "I only listened to part of the book. It's a thriller about a woman who goes to a haunted house in the mountains and *never returns*. Probably too scary for you."

"Is not." Isla yawns, curls up on my bed, and rubs her eyes. With her light blonde hair and rosy cheeks, she looks like a kid from a nineties sitcom. Everyone knows we're sisters with just one glance, except that my hair is dyed a rose-gold color. I still relish the memory of the stricken look on my mom's face after that salon appointment.

I sit next to her and press play on a B horror movie. The opening scene appears and I try to focus on the movie and not on the disaster that awaits me these next few months.

"I can't believe we're spending the *entire* summer in Europe. It's going to be amazing!" Isla's voice is light and excited, like nothing is wrong.

Like my parents never told her.

"We can eat all kinds of yummy pastries and pies. My friend Cindy said that Portugal has the best candy. And think of the ways we can avoid Mom and Dad. And the beaches! I heard—" Isla's unstoppable now, smiling, gesturing wildly as she tells me about all of the things she found for us to do online. Tours, shopping, hidden hikes.

My ears ring and my stomach turns over. My parents didn't bother to tell her. They were leaving that piece of dirty work to me. Probably as punishment.

"La…" I trail off, my stomach twisted into knots. "I'm not coming to Europe this summer."

"WHAT?" Isla slams my laptop shut, her blue eyes flashing with thinly veiled anger.

My stomach twists further. I can't bring myself to face her, so I look at my hands instead. "It's Mom and Dad. They don't want me to come."

"Why not."

It isn't a question. Isla knows why not. She knows about my history with our parents. I stay quiet, wishing that the floor would open up and spit me out somewhere else.

After too many minutes of uncomfortable silence, Isla drags herself off the bed.

"You always do this, Bree. Always." Her voice sounds exhausted, like she's seen one too many things in her twelve years of life. "I was counting on you this summer. I wanted us all to be there together."

"I wanted that too—"

"Well, it's too late now. We're leaving tomorrow. You couldn't keep it together for one more day?"

My shame threatens to swallow me whole.

Isla shakes her head. "Is there even a point in having a sister if she's never around?"

Tears sting my eyes and my cheeks burn. My throat feels raw. I want to say something — anything — but my words will only make things worse.

With a sigh, Isla leaves my room.

The quiet is loud and intrusive and horrible. The screaming has stopped downstairs and I almost miss it.

I sit stiffly on my bed for what feels like hours as sadness and shame sweep through me. I had hopes for this summer. I wanted to see if we could finally, *finally*, be a family. You know the kind — they have dinners together, laugh together, talk to each other like equals. Now, I won't have the opportunity.

Instead, I'll be spending my summer in a big, wooden building without character or magic. I used to spend my summers at Legacy Inn as a kid. Back before my parents started expanding their business and acquiring Mist Mountain Inn, Edelweiss Inn and all the others. I always wondered why they prioritized them over us.

Screw it. I can't sit here any longer. I'm going for a drive.

3

NOAH

A car screeches around the corner, jolting me from my exhaustion. Bright blue headlights race towards me. I'm in the middle of a pedestrian crosswalk, but the lights aren't slowing down.

Fear crawls down my spine as the car closes in.

I dive out of the way.

The car flies past.

I shout a few four letter words at the tail lights of the SUV. It's after midnight, but that's no reason to be speeding through Edendale. I try to memorize the license plate, but within moments, the car is out of sight.

My heart rate normalizes and I shake myself off. Lowering my shirtsleeves, I walk home, wishing I had ridden my Bonneville T100 motorcycle instead.

Unfortunately, the night doesn't get easier. Our house was hit by a tornado.

I step over the shoes in the entryway, spotting the sweaters, notebooks, and make-up items strewn over the living room. Definitely the work of Hurricanes Victoria and Grace. Today was our last day of school at Edendale High, and my twin sisters celebrated by emptying their backpacks across our house.

"Holy, Noah, you look homeless." Grace stands in the corner of the disaster, biting into a sandwich. Her long hair is tied up in a ponytail and her blue eyes are lined with the ever-present black eyeliner.

"Hello to you, too," I mumble, rolling my eyes.

"Your hair, stupid. Come with me."

I follow Grace into the bathroom. She pushes me onto my knees, grabs a pair of scissors, and starts snipping. I look at my reflection as she goes to town on my shaggy black hair. My blue eyes look faded and tired, and my skin is tanned. All those days working on the patio at Spruce Tree have given me a nice base for the summer.

Grace pinches my hair between her fingers, measures it, and makes another cut. "How was your shift?"

"The usual. What're you doing up so late?"

"Prepping for work tomorrow." Grace frowns in concentration and the scissors snip away. "And Victoria is hogging our room. Reading or whatever."

I half-smile at my reflection. When they were younger, my sisters were truly identical and they loved it. Now, they do everything they can to define their identities as separate from one another. Victoria is shy, quiet, and on a first name basis with Edendale's librarians. Grace, on other hand, wants nothing to do with schoolwork. Clothes are her bread and butter, and her favorite pastime is talking about fashion. Or telling me how homeless I look.

There's footsteps outside, then Dad pops his head into the bathroom. "What's happening here?"

Grace jumps slightly at the sound of my dad's voice, and makes an unexpected cut. She glares at Dad. "That's your fault."

A chunk of hair drifts to the ground. A little too much hair. "This is what I get for letting you give me a haircut."

Grace jabs me with her elbow and grabs another fistful of hair. "You had too much hair anyway."

Dad laughs warmly, his grey eyes crinkling on the sides. He smells like pine and sawdust — he must've just gotten home from a job. "How was your last shift at Colman's, kid?"

"Pretty good." I let the words settle. "But it isn't my last shift."

"What do you mean?" Dad's eyes meet mine in the mirror

I immediately look away. "I can't leave you guys here alone all summer."

"You *are* the only thing holding this family together." Grace laughs and rolls her eyes. She squirts my hair with a spray bottle, then runs a comb through it.

Dad sits in front of me so I have no choice but to look him in the eyes. "What about Legacy Inn?"

I shrug. "It's not a big deal. I told Delia that I might not be able to come back this summer. She seemed cool with it. Besides, Spruce Tree and Colman's will be happy to have me working full-time over the summer. It's a win-win."

Dad raises his eyebrows, arms crossed. "For who?"

The bathroom is silent as I scramble for an answer. This is the best way to keep everyone happy, especially my family. But Dad won't want to hear that. Instead, I blurt the first thing that comes to mind. "I can't leave you guys without a babysitter or anything."

At this, Grace's expression makes it clear that she might stab me with the scissors. "Babysitter?! What are we — twelve?"

Dad laughs. "She's right, Noah. You've worked too hard

lately. Great grades, two jobs, and helping take care of your sisters? It's time you escaped this place, get back to Legacy."

"Yeah, haven't you heard? You're looking at the new Sales Associate at Crush Clothing." Grace measures out my sideburns, then nods, satisfied with herself. My head feels about twenty pounds lighter. "I'll accept my fee in the morning. Lucky for you, brothers get half-off of haircuts."

"Great," I say. "What's half-off of nothing?"

Another glare. "Fine. This one's free. But only because Dad startled me."

"Excuses, excuses."

"Brothers." Grace shakes her head, then twirls out of the bathroom.

I stand and run my fingers through my short hair. The truth is, I'd love to go to Legacy this summer. I turn to leave.

Dad casually extends his arm, blocking the door. "Kid. You're going to Legacy. And it's going to be great."

"But—"

"Do you think this is a debate?" Dad smiles. "You need it, Noah. I'm making you do something for yourself for a change. You'll have a great time."

I can't argue with Dad. A tentative feeling of relief washes over me. "Always do."

He pats me on the shoulder. "Your mom loved it there too."

"I remember." My eyes sting as the happy memories threaten to come back. Dad rarely talks about Mom's passing. She died two years ago and the loss was devastating for our family, but especially hard on him. When she got sick, it brought us all to our knees.

But we worked together. We got back up again.

There's no point in getting emotional. I take a deep breath and regain my composure.

Dad smiles. "Do me a favor and have some fun this summer."

"What kind of a favor is that?" I ask, rolling my eyes.

He laughs and gives me a hug. I say good night and head to my room, but instead of going to bed, I take a seat in my desk chair.

I fiddle with a stapler and an eraser. I adjust the angle of my desk lamp. Most importantly, I try to ignore the familiar feeling of dread.

Finally, there's nothing left to shuffle around. With a forced resolve, I stare at the blank page in front of me. The pen in my hand feels like a horrible tactile reminder of the countless nights that I've sat in this exact position.

Someday, I hope to fill the paper with rambling pen scratchings. But tonight, my vision blurs and my brain lulls to a stop.

It's two in the morning and I'm fighting for words that never come.

4

BREE

"*He* approached her with a machete raised high, ready to strike..."

I careen towards the foothills outside of Edendale. I use my teeth to tear open another fruit roll-up package, and then pop the tasty roll into my mouth. Steering with my knee, I press the button to change the radio station. I tune into NWR and wait to hear of any severe weather.

Nothing. If I'm honest, though, even a storm won't cheer me up. With a sigh, I switch back to my audiobook. Listening to scary stories isn't nearly as thrilling when the sun is shining and the sky is blue.

Has Isla read my note yet? Before leaving, I slipped a note under her door saying goodbye. I couldn't face seeing her again. Her, or anyone. I snuck down to Garth and left before sunrise.

I'm halfway through my fruit roll up when a brilliant thought arrives. What if I skip out on Legacy Inn?

The thought makes me giddy.

Does anyone at Legacy Inn even know I'm coming? Or could I turn around and go back to Edendale? I could spend the summer in our big, empty house, listening to my audiobooks, watching scary movies, and chasing storms whenever I want. Some kids from Edendale High might be sticking around for the summer, and they can come over for movie nights.

This summer can be whatever I want it to be. The thought of being free of impossibly high expectations, tedious events, and late-night arguments fills me with an indescribable joy.

Then, on the left, I spot a gravel road and I take it as a sign. Before I can talk myself out of it, I lift my foot off the gas and signal to turn. A forest of thick trees, lit bright green by the sunlight, opens in front of me. In the far distance, snow covers mountain peaks.

This is it. I'm going to spend the summer doing whatever I want in Edendale.

I sit on the side of the road and smile. Another breath, and I'll complete my U-turn and head back to Edendale. Nothing could wipe the smile from my face. Sure, it's not like I'm spending my summer in Portugal, but a summer at home? By myself? Unlimited 'me' time with no responsibility? What could be better than that?

My phone pings. I check the message, hoping it's one of my friends from Edendale.

Nope. It's Delia.

Delia: Hi Bree! It's Delia from the Lethargy Inn. Kate emailed your number to me this mountain. This phone doesn't work properly so I'm not sure I have it right. Anywho. Would you be able to pick up some chanting mink on your way? Keep the recipe. Ciao!

Sounds like auto-correct had a hand in that one.

I don't know much about Delia. My parents hired her years ago when Legacy was struggling. They describe her as a "character" and, the times I met her, I liked her. Given Legacy's success since she joined, my parents have pretty much relinquished control and let her run it.

I sit back in my seat, contemplating the options. On the one hand, I can be "responsible" and help Delia out. On the other hand, I can pretend I never saw the message and go back to Edendale.

Then, my phone pings again.

Delia: *Legacy, *morning, *chocolate, *milk, *receipt. Darned auto-correct

If Delia's struggling with auto-correct, she must be completely overwhelmed at Legacy Inn. She could probably use the help. It's not a massive detour to get her some chocolate milk before heading back to Edendale. I have the whole summer, after all.

Bree: I'll pick up some chanting mink — sorry, chocolate milk — on my way. See you soon.

I throw my phone onto the passenger seat and get into gear, turning onto the highway towards Legacy Inn.

I'll grab the chocolate milk, make a quick stop at Legacy, and inform Delia that I won't be staying. I'll be back in Edendale in no time at all.

5

NOAH

I park my motorcycle in the staff lot and unstrap my duffel, breathing the mountain air. Memories rush back. Hours spent swimming in the lake, exploring the forest, hiking the mountains. Sunburns, hotdogs sizzling over campfires, mosquito bites. To me, Legacy Inn and summer are synonymous, to the point where I started working here after Mom died.

I stroll up the gravel path towards the summer student cabins at the edge of the property. None of the Edendale kids have arrived yet — which means I get first pick. The A-frame cabins are arranged in a semi-circle to house the five student workers. Though, oddly, a sixth cabin has been added to the group this year.

I enter my favorite cabin — the one on the far left — and drop my bag. Over the last few years, the student positions at Legacy have boomed in popularity with the Edendale High crowd. I'm grateful to Delia for saving a position for me every summer. This morning, I was up absurdly early thanks to radio Twin Tornadoes. Victoria and Grace were fighting over a shirt and it was the perfect excuse to get my butt out of there.

I get changed and head to the kitchen. Time to catch up with some of my favorite people.

"Guess who's back!" I push open the kitchen door.

Fernando whips around and runs towards me, enveloping me in a bear hug. He's around the same height as me — a solid 6'1" — but his personality makes him feel a foot taller. "Ciao! Ciao! Noah, you look fantastico. Even look like you have a bit of muscle on you."

"Started working out," I say. "Thought you might be getting a little old to lift the flour sacks without throwing your back out."

Fernando laughs and gives me a fist bump, his dark eyes twinkling. "The boy gets his first muscle and thinks he's a man."

"I think that's one more than you have?" I grin. "It's good to be back, Fer. Where's Carrie?"

"Cheeseburger tacos on the menu tonight, amico!" Fernando says. "It'll be a big hit!"

I tie an apron around my waist. The kitchen, in true Legacy fashion, has a little bit of everything, everywhere. Fernando assembles homemade taco shells, chattering on about the Inn and the drama I missed over the winter. He delicately tries to stack one of the taco shells and it breaks. He swears loudly in Italian. There's the spark — Fernando only gets angry when it comes to food.

"You want a hand, or were you planning to serve all of the tacos deconstructed?" I jump in to help, not wanting Carrie to see me standing idly by. Carrie is the sous-chef, but where Fernando is kind and calm, Carrie is fiery and opinionated. They work extremely well together, like two sides of the same coin — he's the creativity and the inspiration, and she brings the practicality and action.

"One moment, amico. Delia wanted to know what we'll be serving tonight at the Welcome Bash." With a wink, Fernando ducks out of the kitchen. Seconds later, I hear Delia's trademark squeal.

I carefully place a stack of taco shells onto a tray, then exit the kitchen.

"Okay, so Carrie won't be ba— Noah!" Delia's kind face breaks into a warm smile. With her work jeans and colorful top, she's always reminded me of a fun aunt. She flies over to me and wraps me in a hug. "Dearest Noah, how are you?"

"Now that Fernando's left me alone with the tacos, I'm full."

Fernando's face drops and I give him a wink. We burst into laughter.

"It's great to have you back, my boy!" Delia tips her cowboy hat dramatically. "I hope you're ready to help with this evening's Welcome Bash. You remember how important these gatherings are for our newcomers. This year's should be a resounding success. I've got jobs for everyone. Of course, seeing as Carrie won't be here until next week—"

I freeze. "What? Carrie isn't here?"

Delia shakes her head, while Fernando picks obsessively at a spot on his apron. "Carrie is on vacation. Did you not know?"

I shake my head. "Must've missed that."

"Oh Delia." Fernando pipes in, smiling. "You worry *way* too much. Noah and I are fine. Besides, we can steal one of the other student workers to fill the gaps if needed."

I smile weakly. I left two jobs back at home, and I was hoping to relax. But if it's only me and Fernando in the kitchen, I'll be working three times as hard at Legacy.

"Certainly." Delia beams, trying to seem encouraging. "But of course, the other students will be kept very busy..."

Delia trills on about the piles of work she'll be heaping onto the unsuspecting student workers, but my mind wanders. Fernando, Carrie and I can barely cover the basics when things are busy. The thought of just two of us for a whole week, not to mention the first week of summer... It's going to be crazy.

"I'd better get back." I excuse myself, my voice distant.

Fernando and Delia continue their conversation and I hear another screech of delight before I enter the kitchen. "A cheeseburger taco? I LOVE IT!"

I stack another set of taco shells and think of a game plan for the week ahead. For some reason, Dad's words from last night pop into my head. I smile sadly as I remember the "favor" I owe him.

Duty calls and fun can wait.

6

BREE

I breathe the fresh mountain air. A hint of pine and a touch of fresh grass carry through the parking lot at Legacy Inn. It really does smell better here.

My stomach grumbles. I look longingly at the bottle of chocolate milk resting in the passenger seat. It's mid-morning, and I haven't eaten, but I won't be staying at Legacy for long. Fifteen minutes from now I plan to be back on the highway, blasting music, and speeding towards Edendale.

I grab the chocolate milk and head for the front door.

Whoa. Legacy Inn has changed. When I was a kid, the Inn consisted of a squat wooden building with a horrendous seventies style. Now, two guest wings protrude off of the main building, which now looks like an enormous log cabin. The planters full of flowers, the trees and the bushes really do create that "magical mountain Inn" vibe that guests rave about.

I climb the steps. The mountain breeze carries the smell of fresh bread. Birds chirp loudly in the trees. Then, something strange happens — an eerie sense of calm flows through my veins.

I must be light-headed from hunger. I shake myself off and enter.

On the outside, Legacy Inn is serene as a postcard. Inside? Different story. Staffers hustle around the event room. Tables and chairs are scattered haphazardly. The floor is littered with papers and other decorations. A lone string of fairy lights frames a window on the far wall before trailing, abandoned, into a cardboard box.

"Randy, would you be so kind as to grab some waters from the bar?" A loud voice carries above the muttering in the room. A flash of color catches my eye. A woman with a flowing top and work jeans wanders into the room.

Delia.

I jog across the room, trying to keep up with her as she floats towards the balcony.

"Delia!" I call before she can walk through the door. "I have what you're looking for."

"I highly doubt that, dear, but let's see what we can do." She turns around and her smile widens substantially. "Bree Lewis!"

"That's right." I'm slightly out of breath. This lady moves fast. "You summoned me for chanting mink?"

She laughs and swats at my shoulder like we're old friends. "I've tried to turn that dang auto-correct off so many times... but thank you, dear. I did ask for that. We don't need it anymore, our shipment arrived a few minutes ago."

"Happy to help...?"

She places the bottle on a table and picks up the abandoned string of fairy lights. I open my mouth, ready to make my excuse and exit, when she cuts me off.

"Fantastic, I have a *very* exciting position for you." Delia steps on a chair holding the end of the fairy lights and hands me a section to untangle. Within moments, we're working together to string up the lights. "It's highly desirable work, very prestigious. Your parents said you like to be where the action is. That's why I'm giving you the most exciting job!"

That gets my attention. Heart of the action? Exciting job? What could it be? My mind fills with possibilities. Maybe we need to document some astronomical event, or coordinate with celebrities, or dive for treasure in the Legacy Lake. Maybe it'll involve storm chasing?

"You get to be..." Delia pauses for what I assume is dramatic effect. "The receptionist."

My wonderment and curiosity are replaced with overwhelming indifference. So much for exciting. Receptionist? What could be more boring than that?

"Wow," I say, trying to keep the sarcasm from seeping into my tone. I hand her another untangled section of lights. "What a great opportunity, Delia. Unfortunately, I have to—"

"It really is! Now, I do already have a task for you."

"That's great, but you see—"

"As my receptionist, you'll be in charge of handling various guest issues and concerns."

"Sounds cool, but—"

"With the Welcome Bash tonight, I'm afraid I won't have time to review the list of arrivals for tomorrow. I'm trying to make this event the best it can possibly be for our new student workers. We appreciate you all *so* much. Would you be able to prepare the guest list for me?"

My excuse is on the tip of my tongue, but I can't speak the words. Delia's asking for help again. I glance around the room and take note of the frantic action. The stress and tension are palpable.

Can I really leave now?

"Sure," I say weakly, defeated.

"Amazing!" Delia swings her hands around, almost decapitating me with a rogue section of fairy lights. Unable to loop the string over the nail, she sighs, hops off of the chair, and tosses the lights aside. Abandoned. "*And*, not to be the bearer of gossip, but rumor has it that Kade Monroe will be staying this summer with his son, Cooper."

My ears perk up. Kade Monroe is one of Montana's most famous exports. He stars in that big action movie franchise, whatever the name is. A movie star staying at the Inn could be a game changer. The film will have directors, casting agents, a camera crew... Maybe they'll be flitting around the property. Imagine if I get 'discovered' at Legacy Inn.

Get discovered for what, I don't know. Hopefully they can tell me.

"Why don't you grab your things from your car and meet me in reception? Unfortunately, because this all came up at the last minute, we don't have a cabin for you. However, Vin and I are thinking of placing you in a guest room, or maybe a tent. I'll meet you there." She turns on her heel and floats towards the kitchen.

"No." My voice echoes through the room.

Delia slows to a stop, turning with a confused look on her face.

"No," I say again, quietly this time. "I'll stay in the loft."

Delia's eyebrows shoot up in surprise. "No one has set foot up there in years. The last person was... well, it was likely yourself. Are you sure, dear?"

She scoffs like the loft is a relic, a long-forgotten legend from a bygone era. But I've never been more sure of anything. If I'm staying anywhere at Legacy, it's going to be the loft.

"I'm sure." I smile.

"Suit yourself, dear. Go get your things, set yourself up, and then meet me in the reception." With that, Delia continues on her journey, disappearing into the kitchen.

As I grab my pillows, blankets and storm-chasing gear from my car, my stomach flips. My smile is slowly replaced by a frown of bewilderment.

What just happened? I expected to make an excuse, get back in my car, and drive to Edendale. I was going to spend my summer in peace, listening to my audiobooks, chasing storms, and watching scary movies.

My gear stacked in my arms, I open the door to the loft staircase and turn on the light. I climb the old wooden stairs. It's pitch black in the loft, and there's a vague smell of mothballs and dust. I sneeze into my pile of pillows. The floor creaks beneath my feet. I can't remember where the main lightswitch is, so I drop the pillows and blankets on the floor and head for the beam of light peeking through the curtains.

Great. I'm sleeping in a dusty loft with a lofty job as receptionist for the Legacy Inn.

I'm not sure what I've done, but at least as long as I'm in the loft no one will bother me.

7

NOAH

*M*y shoulders and back are tense as I stir the taco meat. My stomach grumbles loudly but I'm hardly aware of it. Fernando is in the event room, clearing plates and mingling with staff. He insisted that I eat lunch with the rest of the staffers, but, with Carrie gone, I know I'm needed in the kitchen.

I'm barely holding down the fort for tonight's Welcome Bash. Between monitoring the taco meat, preparing the salads and getting the lasagna ready, I've hardly had time to check the clock, let alone eat something. All I know is that it's way past lunchtime. I grab a fry from beneath the heat lamp.

Then, like a prayer answered, the kitchen door opens and a guy from school wanders in — Jon or Johnny or something. I know he plays for the Edendale Eagles, but I don't really keep up with school sports.

"Hey, I'm Jonathan," the guy says with a friendly smile. "Delia sent me here. What can I do to help?"

"Noah," I crunch on a fry. "Fernando should be back soon and he's got a list."

Jonathan grabs a spare apron and looks around for something to do. Immediately, a small wave of relief washes over me and my shoulders relax infinitesimally. At least we have another helper for now. I just hope we can keep up. I continue stirring the taco meat and my stomach emits the loudest grumble known to mankind.

Jonathan blinks. "Dude, have you had lunch?"

"No rest for the wicked."

"You need to eat. I'm not much of a cook, but I'm pretty sure I can stir meat."

My stomach grumbles in agreement. I hand over the spoon. "Thanks."

I grab a couple of eggs and bacon, and Jonathan and I talk while I make lunch. It turns out, he not only plays for the Edendale Eagles, but he's actually their star midfielder.

He stirs the taco meat. "Play any sports?"

"Football and basketball back in the day — haven't played much in the past few years." I shove some eggs into my mouth. It's hard to find time for sports when you're working two jobs and helping your dad look after the twin terrors. "Just haven't had the time."

Suddenly, Fernando barges into the kitchen. His eyes are wide with fright. "There's something upstairs!"

"Like a monster?" I ask, a piece of bacon falling from my mouth.

"Worse." Fernando looks at us both seriously. "I think it's a raccoon."

Jonathan and I exchange a glance, then we both burst out laughing.

Fernando glares.

I shake with laughter, nearly choking on my food. "A raccoon?"

"Or something!" Fernando says. He gestures animatedly. "There's a lot of creaking... something is up there."

Grinning, I remove my apron. "I'll deal with your monster, Fer. I used to hang out there all the time when I was a kid."

"Grazie, Noah. Please. Get rid of it." Fernando hands me a broom.

"What do you want me to do with this?" I ask. "Sweep it under the rug?"

"Whatever you need to do," he says ominously.

I roll my eyes. I'm neither sweeping the thing, nor doing whatever Fernando is alluding to, but I can tell he's worried. I grab the broom to appease him, and leave the kitchen. The door to the loft is right next to the kitchen.

Strange — the light in the staircase is on. How long has that been on for?

Something rustles upstairs.

The hair on the back of my neck stands.

The floorboards creak. Whatever's up there must be big. Goosebumps prickle my skin.

I climb the steps quietly, not wanting to alarm the raccoon. At the top of the stairs, I step lightly into the loft. My eyes haven't adjusted to the darkness, but the rustling is getting louder. I hear a noise near the window.

There's something there. Something by the curtains.

Something huge.

I lift the broom. My legs tense, ready to lunge forward—

The curtains lift.

Daylight blinds me.

"Agh!"

At my yelp, the thing screams too. It falls against me and I step back onto something uneven and unstable. Off-balance, I tilt backwards, my arms wrapping around the thing.

I hit the floor, but it isn't hard and painful. I've fallen into a pile of clouds.

I open my eyes and stare into a turquoise gaze that I know very well.

"What the? Noah?" Bree Lewis has fallen on top of me and my arms are wrapped tight around her. Her hands are pressed against my chest and a stack of pillows and blankets has broken our fall.

Bree Lewis. The girl who is as much a part of my summer memories as sunburns, popsicles by the dock, and barbecued burgers.

"Um, surprise?" My voice is gravelly.

"Why are you sneaking up on me?" She narrows her eyes, her voice cautious.

"We can talk when you take your elbow out of my stomach."

"Whoops." Bree peels herself off me and helps me up. A swirl of dust floats in the beam of sunlight, and it makes her look like a vision from another life, like an old polaroid. Which, I suppose, she is. She's wearing jean shorts and a lacy white top, her rose-colored hair falling delicately around her shoulders. She puts her hands on her hips. There's a slight smirk on her lips. "So. What's a boy like you doing in a place like this?"

"Hunting raccoons."

"Raccoons?"

"Fernando thought you were a raccoon."

"What gave me away?" She raises her hands in front of her and twiddles her fingers like a hungry raccoon.

I laugh. "Just keep your paws out of the kitchen and we won't have any problems."

Bree laughs with me, and the sound pulls me into the past. Entire summers flash before me. Capture the flag. Hide and seek. Eating burnt popcorn and watching bad movies. It was a happier, brighter time. Back when we were best friends.

I feel like I'm going to lose my balance again, but Bree doesn't seem to notice.

"I wondered if you might be here this summer," she says. From the tone of her voice, it's impossible to detect whether that's good or bad. "Delia says I was probably the last person to use the loft."

"You weren't," my voice is firm, almost accusatory. "I mean, I was."

"Really?" Bree looks uncertain. She frowns. "Are you sure? Because I—"

"I'm sure." There's a chill in the loft that has nothing to do with the summer breeze, and everything to do with what's happened between us. When I close my eyes, I can ignore it. I can pretend we're still kids listening to the rain patter against the roof and watching movies after a swim in the lake. But when I open my eyes — when I see Bree — I remember what happened three years ago.

I force a smile. "But I'll catch up with you later. I'll tell Fernando his raccoon is much larger than expected."

"And much hungrier," Bree adds.

"Good to see you again," I say. The words have a forced, artificial quality to them. Then I'm out of the loft and down the stairs.

Growing up, I would've stood in front of a bus for her. But after what happened three years ago, there was no point in even staying friends.

8

BREE

"*B*ree, my girl." Nath glides into reception, a living flashback. Nath has been with the Inn for as long as I can remember, her dark hair and twinkling eyes staples of my past. She leans against the reception desk. "I'm heading to the Welcome Bash but wanted to say hi. How're you settling in?"

I shuffle the papers in front of me. "Aside from almost being beheaded by a broom, it's been alright."

"What?!"

"Noah thinks I resemble a raccoon," I say. "Do you think I overdid the eye shadow?"

"The resemblance is uncanny." Nath guffaws and then raises her eyebrows. "Aren't you guys the best of friends?"

Goosebumps appear on my skin. Falling backwards into his arms earlier today opened a portal to our past. My heart was racing from the fright.

"We grew apart..." I trail off, trying to think back over what, exactly, happened to us. "We're different people now."

Noah used to be my best friend — the best friend I've ever had in my entire life. Seeing him at Legacy is eerily familiar but displaced. It's like he's a different person here. Edendale High Noah is the hot, mysterious loner that all the girls crush on. Legacy Inn Noah is my old friend, the keeper of my childhood secrets, the boy who helped me perform the heist known as Operation Fort Legacy.

"I see," Nath says. Her dark eyes pierce through me.

I shift in my seat, feeling oddly like she knows something I don't.

Her eyes clear and she smiles brightly. "Well, we've missed you and we're thrilled you're back. It's going to be a busy summer, Delia is lucky to have you."

With a wave, Nath darts out of the reception.

I return to the list of tomorrow's arrivals. My heart sinks. The more people that see me here, the more difficult it will be to escape. I don't want to let anyone down, but I can't stay here, either. Not if I want to fulfill my dream of a summer just for me. Right now I'm even being — gasp — productive.

Yes, I did it. I put together the list of arrivals for Delia. Kade and Cooper Monroe will be staying in the flashy penthouse, but the rest of the list is a bore. There aren't any other famous people, but if I was Taylor Swift or Emma Watson, I wouldn't be flashing my name around. I would hate to have paparazzi following me. 'Lead actress' might have to stay off my list of career aspirations but, if I work on a movie set, I might consider being a director, or maybe a lighting person...

I haven't put much thought into what I want to do after graduation. The one thing I do know is that I will *not* be attending an Ivy League business school.

The reception is a chamber of silence and I wish there was a radio. But, I won't be here for long, so that's not my problem. I consider napping in my chair, but I've had far too much caffeine. Time for some snooping. Someone as chaotic as Delia *must* have interesting things hidden around her office.

I tiptoe around the reception desk and into Delia's office. A mess doesn't begin to describe what her office looks like. Photos of friends and family line the walls and the shelves. Her desk is littered with paperwork, more photos, and a frog figurine. The aerial photo behind her desk shows the old Inn — the creaky dock that me and Noah used to dive from, the trampoline, the trees where we would build forts.

I continue my tour of Delia's office, snooping in the bookshelves and in her desk drawers. She has a ton of random paraphernalia, including several photos of her skydiving. After discovering tons of party glasses, a couple of guitar strings, a fanny pack with "Edendale Marathon", and a clown nose, I've surmised that there is a *lot* more to Delia than just being the Inn's manager.

And then, I look behind the door. There are cowboy hats — everywhere.

It's a wall of color and each hat is displayed proudly on its own hanger. There are hats with feathers, hats with streaks of rainbow, tie-dye hats, and hats whose rims have bells hanging off. It's the kind of thing you'd only ever see in movies.

I take a rose pink hat off the wall and place it on my head, assessing my reflection in the mirror. Keeping the hat, I check the paperwork on her desk. There are lists and lists of tasks to get done around the Inn, events to run with the guests, weddings to coordinate. It's completely over-whelming.

"Busy bee," I mumble. It's clear why she wants a recep-tionist this summer. I don't blame her for feeling tense and stressed.

I frown and take off the cowboy hat. Delia is not what I

expected. She's wild and lively and colorful, and yet, she's able to run the Inn seamlessly. She brings new ideas to the table, valuable thoughts and perspectives that usually pay off. Or so I've overheard from my parents.

Too bad I won't be sticking around to help. I'm hit with a pang of guilt but I quickly stifle it. Delia has made it this far alone. Surely, she doesn't need me this summer. Surely, I can escape back to Edendale.

I don't want to stay, but I don't want to leave her in a lurch, either. Her to-do list grows longer by the second, and if I add "find a new receptionist" onto the list...

There's only one solution. She has to be the one to send me back to Edendale. If she does, it means that she can handle this herself. Plus, if you believe my mom, I'll probably just be in Delia's way if I stay here. The sooner I make Delia see that, the sooner she sends me home. Win-win.

I place the cowboy hat on its hanger and stroll out of the reception. The bustling chatter and laughter in the event room is getting louder by the moment, signaling the start of the Welcome Bash.

So it's settled. How long will it take for Delia to realise what everyone else already knows: I'm not an asset, I'm a liability.

A few hours later, I'm sitting at a table, my fork plunged into a piece of extra cheesy lasagna. I still haven't figured out a way to prove that I'm a liability. Delia's gathered the staff in the main room and is making announcements. Laying down the ground rules. There's no point in paying attention — she'll be sending me back to Edendale soon.

As soon as I figure out how to make that happen.

I'm mid-bite and considering the best time to drive home when I hear Delia's voice through the crowd.

"Bree Lewis? Where's Bree?"

I turn towards her voice but I can't see anything through the crowd. Delia calls my name again. She wants me to go to the front of the room.

I awkwardly push my way through the crowd of strangers, feeling the eyes of everyone watching me. I don't like being in the spotlight, and especially not in front of people I don't know. My breaths get shallow.

Then, my eyes find Noah's at the front of the room. A sense of calm floats over me as I take my place next to him. He smiles back warmly and I give him a cheeky wink.

He frowns and puts his pinky to the side of his mouth. I continue smiling for a moment before realizing that there's a purpose to this. I slap my hand to my face. When I pull it away, there's tomato sauce on my fingers.

Great. Just great. My cheeks burn.

I wipe off the tomato sauce and sigh. It's a good thing I'm not the kind of girl who's into Noah, or that probably would've killed me. Noah grew up around the time we stopped hanging out and, within a few months, he went from scrawny and awkward to strong and confident. And, he's got really nice hair. When it's longer, it's perfect to run your fingers through. Or so I'd imagine.

I assess him quietly while Delia continues through the list of students. With his full lips and sparkling blue eyes, he definitely isn't bad looking. And he's got that mysterious half-smile that so many girls go crazy for. I wonder what he's thinking about.

Another memory fights for my attention and Delia's voice fades into the background — it's something my mom said years ago.

It was a Saturday and Noah and I were meant to hang out. We had plans to go to a beautiful meadow we used to go to for picnics and day trips. Lying on the grass, our arms outstretched, we could watch storms roll in from the horizon. We stared at the sky for hours, hoping to see ball lightning — where lightning literally forms a ball.

Noah and I both loved storms back then.

Before I was meant to meet him, my mom and I were arguing. She was telling me off for eating the rest of the fruit roll-ups, but I was hungry after a tiny lunch of salad and egg whites — per the latest diet she had me on.

"Where are you going now?" She asked, exasperated.

I tied my blonde hair back into a ponytail. I was wearing this stupid dress she made me put on.

"The meadow. Noah and I are going to hang out for a bit. His mom's dropping us off."

"Don't you think you should get a headstart on your English reading? And what about the Edendale High Tea today?" Her voice was impatient. "Bree. It's time you started thinking about your future."

"I'm thirteen."

"The perfect age to get your act together. Now, take Noah. *He's* responsible, *he's* organized and knowledgeable. *He's* a great kid."

The silence hung in the air, loaded. We both knew what she was implying.

Noah was a great kid. And I was not.

9

NOAH

I shift slightly and my finger brushes against Bree's. I inhale sharply, intensely aware of how close she is right now. She's making it tough to focus on Delia's announcements.

As soon as Delia finishes, I'm scrambling trying to think of something to say to Bree. The memory of having her wrapped in my arms refuses to leave. I can still smell her hair, feel the curve of her spine, see her blue-eyed shock.

But more than that, I'm trying to stifle the wall of memories that threatens to fall over me. Memories of my childhood, our friendship, Mom... It's too much. I want to speak to Bree, to say something. But what?

I open my mouth and take a deep breath, not sure what words will come out. And then Bree jogs away, greeting Jonathan, and I exhale, defeated. Of course Bree wants to chat with Jonathan Wright, the star midfielder. They might even be dating.

But that's not any of my business.

I head over to the kitchen, intending to sneak back in

now that the announcements are over. Fernando has banned me, but there's no way I'm leaving him alone.

The kitchen is full of noise; water bubbling on the stove, the deep fryer sputtering, the stir-fried veggies sizzling. Not to mention Fernando's bellowing along with an Italian pop song.

"Impressive!" I shout when he finishes a particularly high and wailing note.

"ARGH!" He shrieks, jumping around to face me. His abrupt movement causes a chunk of ground beef to drop to the floor. "You're not supposed to be here."

I burst out laughing, then I grab a cloth, ready to clean up the mess.

"Leave it, amico! What was our deal?" Fernando holds up his own dish cloth.

Not breaking eye contact, I wrap my cloth around my fingers. I know what comes next. Fernando takes a swipe at me, laughing, and I leap out of the way. We spend a couple of minutes circling the kitchen, trying to swat at each other.

Finally, Fernando corners me near the door. He swings the dishcloth menacingly and I take a step back. I brace myself for the coming swing, holding my arms in front of myself—

And we're interrupted by Delia fluttering into the kitchen. She grumbles a "hi" and then teeters a box off of a high shelf. She sticks her hand inside and whips out a chocolate bar, barely removing the wrapper before she dives in.

Fernando and I are frozen, the kitchen quiet. Something is clearly wrong. Our chocolate stash is for emergencies only.

"Delia, what's wrong?" Fernando asks after a beat.

Delia takes another bite and leans against the fridge. The happy, smiling, confident lady from moments ago has disappeared — replaced with this gloomy and troubled person. "Nothing we can't handle, I hope."

Fernando immediately drops his cloth. "Dee?"

She stands her ground for a moment, staring back at Fernando. And then, like a popped balloon, she deflates. "It's great news, really. I did the math. This will be our busiest summer for weddings and events."

My stomach drops.

Fernando swallows audibly. "Busier than last year?"

Delia nods.

Last summer was out of control, but the Inn hasn't been able to hire anyone new. If this summer is busier, we'll need to have all hands on deck... and more. I can already feel the weight settle on my shoulders.

Always the optimist, Fernando manages a smile. When he speaks, his tone is warm and soothing. "Don't worry about it, Dee. We have lots of help this year. You have a helper on reception. Carrie will be back soon. We'll make it work. We always do."

Delia smiles tentatively at Fernando's encouraging words. Whether he believes what he's saying or not, Fernando is convincing. Delia nods again and leaves the kitchen, clutching her chocolate bar to her chest.

Then, Fernando turns his sights on me. "What did I say, Noah? It's time for you to go."

Before I can say or do anything, Fernando leaps forward. He grabs my cloth straight out of my hands and starts swiping at me, effectively kicking me out of the kitchen. "Stay out!"

"I'm going!" I scramble away from the whipping cloth.. "Let me know if you need—""

He flicks his dish cloth at me again. "I shall not!"

I roll my eyes but exit the kitchen. I try to hold onto the ray of positivity, but the stress eventually breaks through. My shoulders slump. This summer will be anything but relaxing.

10

BREE

*O*peration: Bree's a Liability is firmly under way as I wander to the table with a plate of food. I have a theory that if Delia sees that I'm alone and miserable, she'll send me back to Edendale. She seems like the type that wants people to enjoy themselves and have a good time.

I just hope I get a chance to talk to Noah before she gives me the boot.

I take a seat at an empty table and make it my business to look miserable and bored.

Delia glances at me and frowns before she's distracted by something else.

Good, I'm making the right kind of wrong impression.

But, my solo seating doesn't last long. Kiara, another Edendale student, eventually comes to sit at my table. I've always been curious about her and her intense love of photography. She's one of those go-getter, driven people with tunnel vision. I can't imagine knowing what I want to eat for breakfast, let alone what I want to do with the rest of my life. I've never wanted anything that badly.

"So, you're the photographer?" I ask after we exchange a

couple of pleasantries. I'm focusing on looking over the room indignantly.

"*One* of them," she responds with a note of bitterness in her voice. "You?"

"Reception." My bitterness matches hers.

She stops devouring her food and we exchange smiles. I think we'll get along.

Then, from the corner of my eye, I see Delia watching us. I cut our conversation short and return to gazing over the room with annoyance, hoping Delia didn't see my smile. I force a bored and unhappy expression, staring dejectedly at everyone around us.

The door to the kitchen swings open and Noah almost falls into the event room. He wanders over to speak with Nath and her husband, and I smile despite myself.

No. Stop with the smiling, Bree.

I stand up and make for the balcony. I need time away from Delia's eagle-eye watching.

11

NOAH

*I*n the event room, the DJ blasts music, and the staffers chat. Everyone is having a good time. I wave at a few old friends before joining Vin and Nath. I'm trying not to think about how swamped Fernando and I will be when the sun rises tomorrow. Stress, for once, can wait.

"Noah!" Nath smiles warmly and kisses me on the cheek. "You clean up well."

"Don't look so surprised." I grin. Nath was one of Mom's closest friends and worked housekeeping with her before becoming the Inn's landscape architect.

"Looks strong, just like his old man," Vin says, slapping my arm good-naturedly. I almost keel over from the blow. Vin used to be in maintenance, but he now acts as assistant manager to Delia. "How's the family, Noah?"

"The twin tornadoes are out of control, as usual."

They laugh. Though they didn't experience the terrible thirteens first-hand, my stories were more than enough for them.

"And your dad?" Nath asks quietly.

"He's... my dad." I answer, shrugging. Luckily, Vin and Nath seem to know exactly what that means.

When I was growing up, Dad used to be incredibly busy with his carpentry business in Edendale. During the summer, Mom would bring me and the twins up to Legacy with her and, despite his workload, Dad always made time to come and visit. After Mom got sick, Vin and Nath dropped by the house a few times to give Dad a hand. Over the years, they tried to stay in touch, but with Dad losing his business and working various jobs around town, it's been tough.

Nath squeezes my hand, a flash of sympathy passing through her gaze. She knows that I don't like to talk about Mom.

Vin changes the subject. "Still writing? I keep telling everyone you're going to be a big bestseller one day. And, if I remember correctly, before leaving last summer, you said you'd have something to show us this year. So, how did it go?"

I said a lot of things last summer. I wonder how many more are going to come back and bite me in the butt? The floor sinks beneath me. I shrug, forcing a smile. "Working on it."

"It'll come," Nath says confidently. Her motherly gaze is comforting, but I look away.

"There's Bree." She pokes Vin in the side. Across the room, Bree walks around the tables. "Can you believe she's back?"

Vin and Nath chatter as I follow Bree's movements. She's changed out of her jean shorts and into a sundress. She moves gracefully, like a dancer or gymnast. When we were kids, it surprised me how quick and strong she was — she always caught me when we were playing tag. And when we tried to balance on rafts in the lake? She was always the last one standing.

Nath brings me back to the present. "I still think you two will end up together."

"You'll never give this up, will you??" I shake my head. Ever since we were kids, Nath has insisted that we were going to have this magic fairytale romance that culminated with a wedding at — where else? — Legacy Inn.

"You two had... something. Something special, like a language no one else understood. Sometimes, it seemed like you could read each other's minds. Bree was an excitable child, but she was calm with you, and I've never seen you smile as much as when you were with her."

Another flash from the past: Bree and I paddling along the lake shore in a plastic tub we turned into a "boat." She talked in a pirate accent the whole time, accusing anyone who wasn't in the water of being a "landlubber." I laughed so hard my stomach ached.

"Fruit roll-ups will do that to you," I say. "We were always just friends. And then nothing."

Even if I did feel something more, I was never going to be good enough for her. It was best that I got a reality check early so I could move on with my life. Not that there was much to move on to... I've dated a few girls and they were all wonderful people, but they never quite fit. Maybe it was the chemistry, or the timing, or something else entirely. I was happy for them to find someone who could give them more than what I had.

"I'll see you guys around." Lost in thought, I head towards the balcony. From the first time Bree and I played hide and go seek, we were never apart. After Mom died, she was the person I most wanted to turn to for support. But it's been years since we had a proper conversation.

I step onto the balcony and take a deep breath of mountain air as the memories threaten to overwhelm me — whispers and snippets of wonderful summer days. I remember her trying to put sunscreen on and squeezing the bottle so hard that the cap shot off, drenching her leg in white goop. She smelled like coconut for the next week.

It doesn't take long to realize I'm not alone.

"Hey Noah," Bree says with a warm smile.

I almost go back inside, but something urges me to stay. For some reason, my heart beats loudly and my mouth dries. The moonlight illuminates her from behind and I'm aware, once again, of how strikingly beautiful she is. I hope that whoever she's dating — whether it's Jonathan or someone else — lets her know it.

"Hey Bree."

My eyes meet hers and the world feels quiet.

12

BREE

*N*oah joins me at the balcony railing and my heart thumps in my chest. We look out over Legacy Lake and our arms almost touch. The moon is bright over the far peaks and the stars are coming out. It's a calm evening, quiet.

"Too much of a party for you in there?" Noah asks.

"Obviously." The sarcasm almost sounds sincere. In truth, I'd love to go back inside and mingle with everyone, but I need to stick with my plan.

Noah knocks his arm against mine and I feel an electric shock — the same I felt when his pinky brushed mine earlier. I hold my breath and I could swear he freezes too. But then, he moves away and it's like nothing happened.

If the girls back at Edendale knew that I was on a balcony, on a moonlit night, next to Noah, they'd practically kill me with their jealous glares. Isabella Hall, in particular. She's a well-known mean girl around Edendale High and, given Noah's hot-but-unattainable status, she's been after him for a while. Too bad he's rejected her every time.

It's weird. Every girl goes crazy over Noah, and yet he

used to be my best friend. I don't know anything about him now, but I still know *him.*

A blast of music reaches us on the balcony, snapping me out of my thoughts.

Noah glances at the party going on behind us. "Delia goes pretty over the top with these Welcome Bashes."

"She seems like the type, judging by her collection of cowboy hats."

"*Collection* of cowboy hats?"

"Haven't you seen The Wall? It's impressive."

"I'm definitely impressed if she has enough to cover a wall."

Our laughter fills the darkness. It's still so easy to talk to him.

"I'll have to sneak you into the reception so you can see."

Noah smirks. "Sounds like a dangerous mission."

"No more dangerous than Operation Fort Legacy."

He nods. "Our greatest success."

A comfortable silence falls between us briefly, only to be interrupted by delighted shouts from the Welcome Bash. It sounds like quite a party. "I remember your mom came up with the idea of the Welcome Bashes so everyone could get to know each other."

I immediately regret my words. Noah and I stopped hanging out shortly before his mom got sick. We've never really talked about it. I hope I didn't overstep.

His mom was the kindest person I've ever known. She was the perfect mom, she embodied home. She supplied us with an endless amount of fruit roll-ups and cheesy chips, followed by copious amounts of carrot sticks and celery.

But, my favorite thing was watching her eyes light up whenever Noah's dad arrived at the Inn.

She would run and jump into his arms and they would

share a kiss that made Noah pretend to gag but melted my heart. In the summer, they were only apart for a couple of weeks at a time, but it seemed that they missed each other every day. They were, in short, the polar opposite of my parents.

They had the real kind of love — the kind from those romantic movies that I'd never dare admit I enjoy watching. The kind I'll never experience myself because I'm too irresponsible and reckless. Or so my mom says.

How does a person plan a life that she knows she'll spend alone? Answer: make fast, brief friendships. Noah was the exception. We spent every summer day together as kids, playing in the trees, swimming in the lake, sleeping in the loft. Until... something? Why was he so ready to move on?

I don't think I'll ever know and maybe that's for the best.

Noah's been quiet since I mentioned his mom.

Finally, he breaks the silence. "She liked putting them on. She liked getting everyone together, getting them dancing. She used to tell me that you don't really know someone until you've danced with them." He chuckles. "I still don't know what that means."

"Wish I could help you out," I say. "But I'm literally the worst person in the world at understanding parents. Or anything, really."

"Don't be too hard on yourself. You're very intelligent." Noah looks at me seriously. "For a raccoon."

I snort. It's decidedly unladylike, but the sound makes Noah laugh.

"Well, as a raccoon, I think we should have a race. To the food table."

"Is that a challenge?" He asks, his eyes glinting.

I wink. "Beating you was never a challenge for me."

13

BREE

I splay myself across the reception desk, feeling bored and aimless. I stayed up too late last night watching scary movies in the loft and now I'm paying the price. To make matters worse, the silence in the office feels louder than any of the rock concerts I've been to. But, I'm making do without a radio.

I click my mouse a couple of times and glance over the rooming lists once again, hoping, somehow, that I might've missed something interesting. But, I can't see any names I recognize. There's just the double booking next week, but that should get dealt with in the coming days.

Then, a welcome sound punctures the air — the ping from my phone. Oh. The text is from Mom. Greaaat.

Hi Aubrey. I trust you're doing well at Legacy Inn and aren't causing too much trouble for Delia. I wanted to let you know that we've arrived safely, and to touch base about Andrew Stewart. He will be back from Saint Tropez at the end of August and is excited for your little coffee date.

Remember, the Stewart Aviation Company are big players in

*Edendale, so please do me a favor and try to behave acceptably.
I'll get in touch as the date approaches so we can prepare you.*

Love, Mom.

I refrain from throwing my phone across the room. No "miss you" or "love you" or "hope Legacy is treating you well." My mom texts me like she texts all of her employees — cold, uninviting, biting.

Speaking of unappealing, Andrew Stewart has to be the toad-iest of the Stewart family children. Just like they've done with a number of "suitable bachelors," my parents have been trying to set me up with Andrew for months. Many of the "important events" I skipped over the year involved him, but it took a two-minute conversation — and him placing his hand on my butt — to ascertain that Andrew was *not* going to be a good fit.

I fully intend to skip that date in August, no matter what it takes. But I can't be bothered telling my mom about that now.

"Tacos, napkins, grilled cheese sandwiches..." Delia mumbles as she wanders into reception.

I snap upright and then, remembering that I'm supposed to be looking bored, slump in my chair, taking a page from my dad's book.

"Good morning, dear," Delia trills and continues through to her office. "How is the first day of work treating you?"

"Not great to be honest." I follow her into her mess of an office.

"Is it because of what happened with Kade and Cooper Monroe this morning?" Delia fiddles with a bouquet of fake roses on her desk. "I told you, dear, if you wanted to see them check in, you had to be here early."

"It's not that," I say, sighing deeply. I'm laying it on thick;

Delia should send me to Edendale after this. "Legacy just isn't *fun* for me."

"You know what *would* be fun? Taking these boxes of napkins to the kitchen." She kicks two boxes over to me as she rifles through a handful of to-do lists.

She's not getting it. I clear my throat and try again. "I'm not sure it would be."

Delia peers at me over her half-moon glasses.

I hold her gaze. Whoever breaks eye contact first loses.

She dances over the mess on her office floor without tripping or breaking eye contact. She stands close — too close — and her green eyes are piercing.

I feel myself faltering, but I can't look away.

Her voice is low. "In life, things aren't always fun. But you have to do them anyway. I hired you for this job this summer and I expect you to do your work, even if it isn't always *fun*. Understand?"

We stand, silent and still. Two statues in a face-off. She's committing to this? There are a billion other things for her to do. But she's locked in a stare-down with a teenager.

My eyes are dry and the urge to blink is overwhelming. I hold my breath and keep my face neutral.

I feel it coming.

Blink.

I drop my gaze, my eyes watering.

Delia taps my shoulder. "Chin up, Bree. I felt the same way at your age, but it really isn't so bad."

I pick up the boxes and frustration bubbles within me. So much for that plan. I could not have been any more direct with her about how I was feeling. So why hasn't Delia sent me back to Edendale?

"Back soon," I mumble.

"Woah, bella! Watch where you're going!"

The boxes of napkins are stacked high in my arms when I wander as gracefully as I can into the kitchen. I shift the boxes to find the owner of the voice. "Fernando. It's been so long!"

Fernando peeks his head over the boxes. "Bree!"

He grabs the boxes and places them firmly on the counter. Then, before I can say a word, he gives me a bear hug.

I laugh, blushing. "Great to see you too!"

The fridge door bursts open and Noah marches out. "Look who decided to show up!"

"The raccoon, you mean?"

"Naturally."

Noah bends over one of the stainless steel counters. He carefully applies mayo to the sandwich bread, his face creased in concentration. What must it be like to be so focused, so dedicated to something — even something so ordinary as mayonnaise?

I remember my mom's words — "Noah's a great kid." The very opposite of everything I am. I've heard through the Edendale High grapevine that he works multiple jobs on top of his schoolwork. Imagine, being that consistent, reliable and organized.

A wicked thought comes to me. My mom would be so pissed if she heard that I was bothering Noah. She'd hate the thought that my wild and careless ways might rub off on him. As an irresponsible person, wouldn't that fit perfectly with my M.O.?

I don't need to destroy his work ethic, but maybe I can

swing it *just* enough to get a rise out of him. It's worth a try, I'm bored today.

"Whatcha doing?" I taunt him.

He smiles his half-smile, cool as a cucumber. "Thought it was clear."

I pick up a pickle.

"This looks really good." I hold the pickle to my lips, about to bite down. "Hope it's okay if I eat it."

"Suit yourself," Noah says.

I bite into the pickle. The taste of vinegar fills my mouth.

He casually adds, "that one might taste a little like the floor."

My eyes grow wide. My stomach lurches. Ew, ew ew! I run to the sink and spit out the bite, throwing the pickle into the garbage disposal.

I can almost taste the floor — whatever floor tastes like. "You could've said something!"

"You seemed so intent on eating it." Noah places cheese onto a mayo-covered bread slice, unnervingly casual. "And also, it didn't actually fall on the floor."

"Well played." I glare. So that's how it's going to be. Maybe I won't be able to taunt him into submission, but a lifetime of summers together has given me knowledge of his weak spots. His back is to me, so I slip behind him quietly.

As he's placing a slice of cheese on the final piece of bread, I jab at his side. I'm trying to tickle him, but my jabbing motion is a little more aggressive than necessary.

"Ah!" He pulls to the side, an unmistakable laugh escaping. His arm whips out, and, like a frisbee, the slice of cheddar flies across the room. It lands on the back of Fernando's head and stays there for a breath like a square orange hat.

Fernando freezes.

The cheddar falls tragically to the floor.

Uh oh, we went too far.

Fernado stares sadly at the fallen cheese slice. "What a waste of good cheddar."

"Sorry Fernando." We say in unison, both staring at the ground. Through my eyelashes, though, I see Noah smiling, just a bit. My heart races from the adrenaline.

Fernando picks it up, shrugs, and pops the cheddar into his mouth. "Five second rule!"

"Okay, Sawyer." I face Noah and puff my chest out, but he still towers over me. When did he get so tall? "I don't know how and I don't know when. But I *will* get a rise out of you."

Noah's sparkling blue eyes meet mine and I wait for his answer, holding my breath.

"You can try, Lewis. You can try."

14

NOAH

*B*ree and I stare each other down, just like we did when we were kids. She wants a staring contest? I'm determined not to lose. Her turquoise eyes bore into mine and the world feels quiet again. It's just me, her, and this competition.

I smile. Bree always used to do this — press my buttons until she got a rise out of me. I was the level-headed one in our duo and she found it really entertaining when I lost my cool. What's she going to cook up in that sharp brain of hers?

Then, Fernando's ringtone breaks the spell.

"Oh, I must get this!" He answers the call and exits the kitchen.

I'm suddenly aware of how close I'm standing to Bree. I see the flecks of gold in her eyes, the slightest of freckles on her cheeks, the bow of her lips. I almost want to tilt down and kiss her—

What? Where did that come from? Cool it.

I clear my throat and step away, getting back on track.

The silence stretches between us, but Bree doesn't leave the kitchen.

"You know what would be really annoying?" I ask. "If you started cutting tomatoes."

A flash of worry crosses Bree's face and she glances towards the door, but she quickly pastes on a beaming smile. "Love to."

I stack the vegetables on the counter while Bree washes her hands. She ties an apron around her waist, then stares at a pile of lettuce, her expression unreadable.

"You must love working in the kitchen." She picks up a knife and examines the edge like she's suspicious of it. "Is being a chef your dream, end-of-the-line, love-this-forever kinda job?"

I laugh at her serious tone. I've never heard anyone speak of their "dreams" in such a grim way. "Legacy's a great place to work. But chopping veggies and setting kitchens on fire will always come second to writing."

I freeze, my hand in the air. Why did I say that?

Bree carefully slices the end off of a tomato. "Still writing stories?"

"Sort of." I cut through a tomato and start to chop, allowing the mindless movement to quiet the crush of despair. Can I even call myself a writer anymore? When was the last time I got words on the page? I've tried so many things to break through the writer's block — meditation being the most recent. But, aside from feeling mildly more relaxed in the midst of my sisters' screeching, it didn't help. "I've been back and forth on a few projects."

"What's your top project? Like, what do you want to write about most?"

I clamp my mouth shut. I've said too much already.

When we were kids, I couldn't control my words around Bree — she had a way of making me speak my mind without realizing I was doing it. Even my stupid ideas didn't feel stupid when she was around.

I don't want to answer the question, so I give a wordless shrug.

A fire lights in her eyes.

My heart sinks.

This is the reaction she was looking for. When it comes to secrets, Bree's a dog with a bone. "Come on, Sawyer. You know you want to talk about it."

I choose my words carefully. "I'm good. Seriously."

"But I'm your oldest friend. Don't you want to tell me what you're writing about?" She blinks her eyelashes innocently.

The simple gesture almost shatters my resolve. But, I steel myself against her blue-eyed stare. "Fernando's going to be back soon. We should get slicing."

Bree frowns and I turn back to chopping vegetables. I sneak a glance at her, and she has a scheming look in her eyes.

Then, unexpectedly, she drops the topic with a shrug. We finish the sandwiches, chatting easily. After a while, I realize that my shoulders aren't tense and my mind isn't racing. It's kind of fun having her around in the kitchen.

"All right, Sawyer." Bree places the sandwiches on a serving tray. She motions with her fingers to say she's watching me. "Until next time."

"Next time you bore me with your presence, you mean?"

"Something like that."

The kitchen door closes behind her and the room is eerily quiet. Strangely, I miss her presence, like the kitchen was brighter when she was here. I wipe the counter but my mind is elsewhere, given to memories of my childhood here with Bree — memories I'd buried so deep beneath grief that they feel like experiences that never happened to me.

15

BREE

"So, your parents own Legacy? What's that like?" Anaya pops the last bite of cereal into her mouth and stares at me expectantly. Stefi and Kiara sit back in their seats, waiting for my answer. I've been working at Legacy for three days now and the four of us have started eating our meals together, almost accidentally.

I've been waiting for this topic to come up, dreading it. Everyone wants to know the dirt about the successful Lewis family.

"It's great. Amazing," I say robotically, staring down at my empty plate.

"I bet it's time consuming for them," Kiara pipes in. She doesn't look like she's hunting for information, or craving gossip.

I relax slightly. "That's an understatement."

Fortunately, Stefi, Anaya and Kiara move on from the subject. In no time, we're chatting about Stefi's freak encounter with Cooper Monroe earlier today. We clear our plates. After breakfast, my cheeks hurt from smiling. Apparently, I'm actually enjoying my time at Legacy Inn so far. Weird.

Heading to reception, I get into gear for mission "slack back to Edendale." The thought came to me last night after another day of feigning complete boredom. If Delia won't send me back because I'm miserable, she has to send me back if I'm a bad worker... Right?

I stroll into reception — the chamber of silence — and Delia is nowhere in sight. I sneak into her office and pluck my favorite pink cowboy hat off the Wall. Placing it squarely on my head, I return to the receptionist's desk and click the mouse a couple of times. The screen with the rooming lists appears but, instead of doing actual work, I open a new tab and search for "Portugal."

After a few minutes of scanning through images, though, the satisfaction ebbs and sadness takes over. My parents are there right now, with Isla — perhaps they're visiting that beach today, or that castle. I've been messaging Isla and she's doing well, but it isn't the same as being with her in person.

The phone breaks the silence and I glance around. No Delia in sight.

"Legacy Inn, this is Bree." My tone is friendly and professional.

"Hi, I was wondering about your services. Your website says there's a lake, I want to make sure that there are life-guards? I have two young kids and..."

Delia strolls into reception and I stop paying attention to the caller. Reflexively, I sit back in my chair, adopting a lazy posture. I hold the phone against my shoulder and check my nails like I couldn't care less about the person on the other end of the line. Then, I tip the pink cowboy hat in greeting.

"Yeah," I say loudly when there's a break in the guest's monologue. "That's right."

My voice is unmistakably disinterested, but thankfully, the guest hasn't caught on. She thanks me and hangs up, but I keep the phone tucked on my shoulder, wanting to play up the "slacker" label. Delia is rummaging in her office and I know she can hear me.

"Yes," I say to the dial tone, feigning impatience. "Didn't I just say that?"

Delia's office has gone quiet. Yep, she's listening now.

"Well, what do you want me to do about it?" I say angrily to the dial tone.

Delia's shadow appears in the door frame.

Time for a flawless finale. Surely *this* will get me sent back to Edendale.

"Then go somewhere else! We're way too busy for you, anyway."

I slam the phone down and wait for Delia to storm out of her office to send me packing.

Seconds go by and nothing happens.

Was my voice too quiet? Did she hear me?

Then, Delia strides out of the room holding a phone receiver in her hand. She heard the whole thing. She knows I faked the end of the conversation.

I look at her sheepishly. What's she going to do about it?

She has a suspicious smile on her face. "You're way too much like me when I was your age."

With that, she returns to her office and I hear her chuckling. I hide my burning face behind my computer screen.

16

NOAH

*T*he kitchen door slams open and Bree saunters in. I smile instinctively and my heart skips a beat. I probably just had too much coffee this morning.

"Fernando, get the broom," I shout, even though he's nowhere near the kitchen. "The raccoon's returned."

Bree leans against the counter, a devilish look in her eye. "Can't a girl drop in unexpectedly on a childhood friend?"

"Only if she has no ulterior motive."

She puts her hand on her chest and mock gasps. "Me? Never."

I meet her gaze and then continue slicing carrots. A minute ago, I was stressing about there being too much to do. Now, I just want to talk to her, find out what she has planned.

"What's that?" she asks, pointing to the container next to me.

"Slime."

"Looks tasty." Without warning, she sticks her finger into the Jello, licks it, and then sticks it back in for another taste. "Super tasty."

I stifle a smile and then paste a bored expression on my face. Little does she know that I abandoned that Jello about an hour ago. I'm not going to pop her bubble though, she's trying so hard.

She frowns at my nonplussed expression and continues walking through the kitchen, no doubt looking for another disruptive opportunity. She spots the radio. "It's so quiet in here. Some music, perhaps?"

"I'd be careful with that." I tip the sliced carrots into a bowl. "Fernando is very particular about which station he plays."

"Really?" she asks with a note of suspicion. "*Fernando* is particular?"

She meets my gaze and her eyes carry a dare. She turns the dial and the volume goes up on some European techno song. Then, she hovers her fingers over the channel buttons.

"Your funeral." I shrug with a smile. Fernando is generally easy-going but he knows what he likes when it comes to music.

As she changes the station, I wonder, idly, what Bree listens to now. Maybe R&B or country. Or pop. The next station is playing a song I love — a classic rock ballad. Immediately, Bree turns the volume way up and starts twirling around the kitchen, singing along and knocking pots and pans to match the instrumental. She spins and dances all the way over to me. I can't keep my eyes off her.

"Come on!" She shouts over the vocals. "We used to love this song. Remember?"

I remember. We used to dance in the garden until our feet hurt and then jump in the lake. I smile and put my knife down, leaning against the counter. I watch her as she continues dancing. She looks so free, so uninhibited.

I'd love to be that free. To have that much fun again.

"MI BELLA!" Fernando charges in and takes Bree's hands. "This is a classic!"

Fernando twirls Bree around, dips her, pulls her back up, and then spins her around once again. By now, I'm whooping and clapping along with them. My face hurts from smiling, the stress from minutes ago a distant memory. But too soon, the song ends and Fernando places Bree squarely back on her feet.

"Wonderful dancing with you, cara mia." Fernando bows deeply, then turns the music back down to acceptable levels.

Bree strolls over to me. Unsure what else to do, I give her a fist-bump. "Well, that was entertaining for a Wednesday afternoon."

"I'm here to entertain." She winks and then leaves the kitchen.

Fernando and I return to our tasks, our spirits higher. It's been tough without Carrie and I'm excited for her to be back. But my stomach knots up anytime I think about the busy weeks ahead. Around Bree, some of that stress melts away.

Bree has always been like that — a flash of lightning. She lives for a spark of excitement, bright and colorful, and then moves quickly onto the next thing. It's the exact behavior that used to drive her parents crazy. But I found her fun, exciting and inspiring. The very definition of an individual.

I tune out of most of the Edendale High gossip, but I've heard a few things about Bree over the years. She's brilliant, but only on her own terms. She'll skip a week of classes, and then show up and ace the exam. Usually. It's amazing this habit hasn't caught up with her yet. From what I can tell, she keeps to herself and doesn't have a designated friend group or clique. She floats from group to group, but everyone speaks of her kindness. I've heard that she's gone on dates with a few guys at Edendale High — mostly the rich, upper-class kids — but nothing stuck.

"Can you get the cake ready for tonight's wedding?" Fernando asks. "We're running behind."

I'm ripped back to the present moment and my stomach knots up again. Peace never lasts long.

"Happy to help," I say automatically, my lifetime motto.

17

BREE

I place the mail on Delia's desk and return to reception, enjoying the soft notes coming from the radio. Yes, I succumbed to the silence issue and brought in a little portable radio. I'm playing it softly and keeping it within reach so I can turn it up whenever Delia enters the room.

It's been a week and, despite mission "slack back to Edendale," Delia has yet to kick me out. I'm still here, still plotting ways to be a bad worker whenever she's around. I'm vaguely aware that there are certain aspects of the Inn that I'll miss when I get sent back to Edendale — like the people and, even, somedays, the work.

But no good will come out of me staying. I'll just mess things up for Delia.

I'm processing the check-ins from the afternoon, humming along with the beat of a song, when a guest flies into the office.

"Excuse me, excuse me!" She's holding young twin girls by the hands. The girls look bored and annoyed, tugging at their dresses. I get an unnerving flashback to my own childhood, when my parents would stuff me into fancy dresses for the most mundane events.

"I want to get a photo of the girls to send home to their dad. Where can I find the photographer?" Her tone is clipped and frustrated.

"We actually have two photographers here at the Inn." I check the window towards the garden and the lake.

"Fine, the TWO photographers." She sneers.

My hackles go up, but I force myself to speak calmly. "You can find Jonathan and Kiara by the lake."

"No," she snaps, and I see the twins exchange a glance of glee. "I don't want a photo by the lake."

I keep my face composed. "I'm sure you can ask them to take a photo elsewhere, but they do have a good sense of the lighting."

One of the girls tugs her hand, her voice excited. "Please, mommy, can we go to the lake?"

The lady shoots me a mean glare before turning towards her child. "Fine, Charlotte. But under no circumstances will you be going in the lake until *after* the photo is taken. Understood?"

Charlotte nods, her expression sour. Oh man, that throws me back.

The lady nods at me, her face impassive. This is probably as close as she gets to a joyful expression. "Fine, then."

She heads out the door, dragging the twins behind her. They look up at me and I give them a wink. When the merry threesome has left the room, I head back to my desk, turning the radio up a couple of notches. I'm grinning. Oh to be a young troublemaker again.

"Well, what do you know?" A voice by the door surprises me.

I freeze. Delia.

"You handled that exceptionally well, dear." She leans against the doorframe with practiced casualness. "That Mrs. Caron is a real piece of work."

My jaw drops. Since I've been here, Delia hasn't said one bad thing about a guest.

"I spoke to her on the phone before she arrived." Delia strolls into the reception and turns the volume up on the radio even further. "She asked me if there was any way to make sure all of our deep-fried food was vegan. Fernando created a vegan menu for her, and then, believe it or not, I saw her gorge herself on the — non-vegan — mac and cheese last night!"

I stifle a laugh, unsure how to play this. Delia caught me... actually being good at my job. Best to backtrack. I need to set low expectations.

"Yeah." I yawn. "I hope I wasn't too rude."

Delia chortles and heads into her office.

I look around while my mind races. How can I save face? I check the time — my break is in five minutes but I'll take it now.

"Off to the kitchen," I shout and then leave without waiting for a reply.

Over the week, I've been sneaking into the kitchen whenever I get the chance, helping Fernando and Noah with odds and ends. Time passes so quickly when I'm hanging out with them, and today, the last kitchen staff member will be arriving — Carrie. I briefly remember her from my childhood as a loud, confident lady.

I giggle thinking about my attempts to get a rise out of Noah. There's been no progress made on that front yet, but I'm enjoying our conversations. He talks about his sisters a lot. Last year, in the midst of a prank war, Victoria found an embarrassing photo of Grace, blew it up until it was gigantic, then had it made into a flag. Which she flew outside their house.

We also talked about his work at Colman's and Spruce Tree, and about the activities I sampled at Edendale High. I tried my hand at baking, woodworking, volleyball, yearbook... Nothing struck me as particularly interesting, though I'll admit I got a kick from adding student "labels" to the yearbook. My favorite was for the Edendale High goalie and resident bully, Lucas Therborn — so-labeled "Eden-jerk." I flitted onto the next thing before printing and sadly my labels were removed.

"Honey, I'm home!" I storm into the kitchen, but my voice can barely be heard over Fernando's wailing. He's singing along to a pop song, and not well. Noah's standing by the griddle, whistling along with Fernando's off-key vocals. Neither of them heard me come in.

My hands tingle in anticipation as a thought comes to mind — the perfect way to get a rise out of Noah. I spot the burger buns, the cheese, the cutting boards, the knives. They'll be needing vegetables soon.

Not wanting to draw attention to myself, I sneak across the kitchen floor. Monitoring the room, I duck behind counters and shelves to avoid detection. Finally, I hide behind a bowl of tomatoes. It's almost time.

Fernando and Noah are distracted by something on the stove.

Now's my chance.

I pop into the walk-in fridge and close the door behind me.

Darn, I forgot a sweater. But it's worth it.

18

NOAH

"*Mi* amoreeeeee!" Fernando bellows. His voice has never been topnotch, but what he lacks in pitch he makes up for with enthusiasm. It's hard not to smile when he's singing.

I flip a burger on the grill and my mind travels back over my first week at Legacy Inn. In one week, I've had more fun than I've had in years. Fernando is always great to spend time with, but having Bree here restores a balance. I guess that's what happens when you're spending time with an old friend.

I'm smiling down at a burger patty like an insane person when I realize that Fernando has stopped singing. I look up and he's staring at me with an amused expression on his face.

"What're you thinking about, amico?"

"That you could use a few more singing lessons," I say quickly. My cheeks are heating up. Am I blushing? No, it's just hot by the griddle.

"Even my singing doesn't make you smile this much,

amico." Fernando grins. "Maybe you're wondering when your girlfriend will make another appearance."

"Very funny." I stare intently at the burger patty and flip it. To my amusement, on the other side, the burger has cooked in such a way that there's a smiley face.

"I've seen the way you look at her, all secret glances and hidden smiles," Fernando says. "You two ever date?"

I laugh loudly, but the blasting radio and the sizzling griddle overshadow my incredulous reaction. "Never. We are, and have always been, just friends."

Fernando gives me a look. "Really? In all of your years 'hanging out,' you've never wanted to date her?"

I pick up the smiley burger on the spatula. "My one and only true love is Betty. Check her out."

Fernando rolls his eyes and I place Betty back on the griddle. When Fernando gets serious like this, no amount of goofing off can steer him off track.

"Even if I *was* interested, she'd never go for me. Her family owns Legacy Inn. She's beautiful and dates the best guys out there. She's way too good for me. And that's fine, me and Betty will have a pleasant life together."

Now, his face breaks into a little smile. "L'amore vince sempre. Love conquers all."

What does he mean by that?

I brush it off. Bree's been gunning to annoy me all week and she has succeeded a couple of times, but I'm well-trained to hide any frustration — having two teenage sisters has done wonders for my tolerance. Plus, the odd times she's not been trying to get a rise out of me, I've enjoyed talking to her.

I feel like I can tell her anything. I never get bored or distracted and I've never wondered, anxiously, if we should get back to work. She's endlessly entertaining with her stories about sneaking out of her house to chase storms, her favorite audiobooks, entering a hot dog eating contest and coming in second. It feels like I know everything about her, but I always want to know more.

I'm about to flip the smiley patty when a welcome voice echoes throughout the kitchen.

"How're my boys doing?" Carrie flies into the kitchen and I could almost shout with relief. She's back!

Fernando and I rush over to give her a hug, asking her all about her vacation. After five minutes of chatter, Carrie has already had enough and is looking around the kitchen determinedly. "What needs to be done?"

The magic words. Fernando fills her in on the busy summer ahead and her face hardens. There's no easy return after her vacation. But, efficient as ever, she dives in, putting together cupcakes for tonight.

My heart singing, I head to the fridge to get lettuce for the burgers. I place my hand on the door, and then notice a tomato on the ground. I pick it up and place it back in the bowl.

The door clicks.

It opens.

And out comes Bree, like a fridge yeti.

I yelp and hold my arms out, trying to catch her as she falls out of the fridge. Behind me, Fernando and Carrie scream.

"RACCOON!" Bree shouts. And then shivers. Her lips are blue.

"What the?!" I yell and Fernando turns down the music. "How long were you in there?"

"L-l-l-ong e-e-enou-gh." She shivers and her teeth clatter together.

She's wearing a crop top and a skirt — not appropriate

clothing for 40F. I grab my leather jacket and cover her shoulders. She's shaking.

"What were you thinking?" I demand, rubbing her arms.

"It-it was just." She shivers again. "Too-too-too good an opp-opportunity."

"I hope it was worth it."

Her eyes meet mine and her eyelashes are just the slightest bit white from the cold. Nevertheless, there's a fire in her eyes that could melt the contents of the fridge.

"Definitely."

19

BREE

*L*ater that evening, I'm marching into reception to sign out after catching up with Carrie in the kitchen. I forgot how spunky and snappy she is with her dyed red hair, big glasses, and boisterous laugh. It's crazy to me that these people — these strangers — sometimes feel more like family than the family I do have.

It's been a long day in a pleather skirt and I'm excited to change into my pajamas. My form of rebellion today was in my attire. My hair is tied up in crazy-looking braids, and my red skirt and black crop top are more suited to a rock concert than work. Sadly, this outfit did not keep me warm during my sojourn in the fridge.

I'm whistling Fernando's favorite song when I stroll into reception. The tornado of movement stops me dead in my tracks.

Two young boys jump on the couches at the far end of the room. Their parents loom over the reception desk, angry and frustrated. They're gesturing wildly to Delia, who types furiously at my computer.

Where I should have been waiting to greet guests.

Uh oh.

I rush into the room. "What's going on?"

Delia peers at me over her half-moon glasses, her green eyes furious. A pit forms in the base of my stomach. I've never seen her mad.

"That's what I'm trying to find out, Bree." Her voice is stern. But worse than that, she sounds disappointed.

I scramble around the desk and look at the computer screen. The pit sits heavier in my stomach. It's the double booking. The one I didn't bother dealing with because I wasn't going to be at Legacy for the fallout.

"Mr. and Mrs. Sharp are under the impression that they have a booking for a two bedroom condo, however, they're currently booked into the same unit as Mr. and Mrs. Brown." Delia narrows her gaze. "I thought this problem was corrected, but apparently not."

The screen swims before my eyes. "I am so, so sorry."

"And is sorry going to fix our problem?" Mr. Sharp asks. "We came all the way from Central Florida to be here. Central. Florida. Do you know how many hours we've been traveling for — with kids? And now, to discover that some stupid receptionist has given away our room?"

His words land like a slap to the face.

Delia immediately stands up. "There is no need to use that language with my staff, Mr. Sharp."

Mr. Sharp, very smartly, clamps his mouth shut and Mrs. Sharp shifts from foot to foot, her expression fiery.

"Bree." Delia turns to me, her eyes flashing but her face suspiciously calm. "Seeing as you got us into this, do you have any suggestions for Mr. and Mrs. Sharp?"

My face burns. I've never felt this way before, not even when my parents scolded me. This feels much more serious and I'm withering under Delia's stern look. The reception is eerily silent, like we've entered a vacuum. Time is ticking. I need to think of something.

"The wedding preparation suite," I sputter.

Delia's face relaxes a fraction but she stays silent.

"It's a beautiful suite." I face the Sharps and put on my best "Customer Service" smile. "The bridal party uses the suite to prepare for the wedding. There are two rooms and it's equipped with a kitchenette."

The ghost of a smile appears on Delia's lips. It's not much, but it's enough to give me confidence.

"There's a Queen bed in one room and, for the kids, we have a couple of comfortable cots available. We can position them by the door so you all have plenty of space." To my delight, the Sharps appear to relax a bit. Time for the final sell. "*And*, the master bath has a jacuzzi tub. No other two bedroom condo at Legacy has one of those."

Mr. and Mrs. Sharp look at each other and exchange a smile. I did it!

"What about the bridal party, Bree?" Delia pops my bubble. "Where do you suggest they get ready?"

My mind races once again. We only have one wedding tomorrow. I frown, puzzling it together. "They're staying in a three bedroom suite. Why don't we offer them additional snacks on the house, and maybe a bottle of champagne?"

I glance at Delia tentatively and her face widens into a smile. She nods.

"That'll be fine." Mrs. Sharp grabs her children's bags. "Thank you."

"I'll take you to your suite," Delia says. "Bree, it's time you told the bridal party about the change of plans."

Mr. and Mrs. Sharp take their bags and file out of reception with their kids in tow. The call with the bride goes better than expected, and when I hang up the phone, I'm smiling. Judging by the cheers and celebrations in the background, the bottle of champagne will be welcome.

I wait with bated breath for Delia to return to reception. She isn't going to be happy with me. But, isn't this exactly what I wanted? I wanted Delia to be mad and send me back to Edendale. So why is it that I want so desperately to stay?

Finally, the moment of truth arrives and Delia strides back into reception. Her voice is not stern or angry, but exhausted. "You've outdone yourself."

"I am so sorry. Truly, I am. I should've paid more attention."

"Yes, you should have." She leans against the doorframe, her green eyes piercing.

I can't meet her gaze.

"Whether you like it or not, you're here for the summer. And that means that, until August, you're part of our little family. So it would be best if you put any anger you're feeling towards your parents behind. For all of our sakes."

My face burns with shame and I stare intently at the desk.

"The truth is, I need your help." Now, her voice is soft. "I need you to work *with* me this summer and not against me. Your lackluster attitude may be your way of getting back at your parents, but what you're doing isn't hurting them. It's hurting me and everyone here. It's time to do better. I know you can." She goes into her office, the door clicking shut behind her.

Her words are falling knives. My eyes fill with tears and shame threatens to bring me to my knees. Delia's seen through me this whole time. She knows exactly what I've been up to.

For the first time, maybe ever, I understand my mom's warnings — my carelessness led to this. Because of me,

Delia is upset, the guests are upset, the staff at Legacy are upset.

"Oh, and Bree?" Delia calls from her office. I wipe away the tears and paste a neutral expression on my face. I open the door to her office and Delia's sitting behind a pile of paperwork. "Please move your SUV out of the guest lot. Guests are beginning to ask questions about the dents and bumps. You can do it this evening, after your shift."

With that, Delia returns to her stack of papers. I close the door and walk out of reception, my cheeks on fire.

20

BREE

I step into the cool evening air and let my emotions consume me. Strangely, the shame and embarrassment is compounded by gut-wrenching fear. This past week, I've enjoyed myself more than I ever could've imagined. Legacy has started to feel like a home, the people like family.

After everything I've done, I don't want to return to Edendale.

Garth is parked in the corner of the guest lot. My banged-up, silver SUV looks rough compared to all of the brand-new sedans, sports cars and convertibles.

I take a seat and turn the key in the ignition. Garth sputters and shakes to life. It feels like it's been a year since I sat in the driver's seat, though it's only been a week. How is it that so much can change in such a short time?

I think about the last conversation I had with my parents, and shivers run down my spine. When I'm in trouble with them, they usually level a punishment at me and call it a day. They never expect much of me because they're used to what I deliver — not enough, in their eyes.

But somehow, after an act of carelessness that could've easily cost the Inn a good deal of business, Delia *still* hasn't given up on me. In fact, she expects more from me, she simply expects me to do better.

That's the scariest thing of all.

I pull out of the guest lot and make my way to the staff parking. I back into a parking spot, but leave Garth running, and stare at the mosaic of clouds above me.

My mind races. Delia expects so much of me. So, so much. I'll surely let her down. She wants help this busy summer, but I'm definitely not her best option. Maybe I should go back to Edendale after all.

My stomach drops to my toes. I only ever mess things up. No wonder my mom says that I'll never have any meaningful relationships. I'm too wild and flighty, too much to handle. Most of my "dates" have been pre-arranged, horribly cringey encounters. At school, I've flirted shyly — and not well — with a few guys, but my mom's words echo permanently in my head and I chicken out before the first date every time. I'll only ever let them down.

It's what I do. The Bree Lewis special.

Anger and confusion consume me. Only one thing can comfort me now. I check my phone and I know where to go.

I'm about to put Garth in gear when I notice Noah exiting the Inn. He walks solemnly to a motorcycle and flips up the rear seat, rummaging about in the storage compartment underneath.

Interesting. I didn't peg Noah for the kind of guy who would have a Bonneville T100. Loads of girls at school mentioned his motorcycle when swooning over him, but I never noticed before.

I get another idea.

21

NOAH

"*C*all it a night, kid!" Carrie's bellow is quickly followed by a slap on the back. I give her a fist-bump and hang up my apron. No point in arguing with Carrie.

She then turns to Fernando. "Where did you say you put the chocolate sprinkles?"

"Where we always keep them."

"So, your stomach?" Carrie says solemnly.

Carrie and Fernando's playful banter follows me out of the kitchen and I roll my eyes. It's great to have Carrie back. Her passion and intensity are a nice contrast to Fernando's milder nature. Not to mention the weight it takes off to have another hand in the kitchen.

The kitchen door slams shut and I'm overwhelmed by the stillness in the event room. Dinner tonight was loud and bustling, typical of Sundays at the Inn. Now, it's getting late and the guests are either enjoying the evening party in the garden, or have already gone to bed.

I wave at a couple of staffers milling about the room, and then, my heart sinks. The nagging thought I've been trying to avoid all week can no longer be ignored. I gave myself the week to settle in at Legacy, and I hoped a few days off would help me push past my writer's block. But, I don't feel any more inspired than I did last week or last month or last year and I can't put it off any longer.

Being a writer has been my dream for as long as I can remember. I started working on a story before Mom got sick, but after we lost her, I scrapped everything. Now, another story has been forming in the back of my mind, but I can't figure out how to get it on paper.

With a resigned sigh, I throw on my leather jacket and make my way to the staff parking lot. I was hoping that being at Legacy might spur some of my thoughts into action. Instead, I still don't know where to start.

I walk through the parking lot and stare intently at the ground, barely noticing the SUV with its headlights on. I lift the rear seat on my motorcycle to get into the storage compartment, preoccupied and thinking of the perfect first words for the first page of my first novel. I grab my notebook and pen.

Across the parking lot, the SUV roars to life, tearing me from my thoughts.

I don't spare it a glance, it's just another staff member off for a late night escape. I expect the vehicle to pull out of the parking lot, but it doesn't. Instead, it lurches towards me, its headlights flashing.

Why is it coming this way?

I hold my hand up to cover my eyes from the glare. It looks like — no, it is — the same silver SUV that almost mowed me over on my way home from Colman's.

The SUV bounces over potholes, coming right at me.

Adrenaline shoots through me. I dive over my motorcycle to get out of the way of the speeding vehicle.

It roars past, almost clipping my motorcycle, then stops. The engine dies. There's a steady buzz as the window rolls down.

Bree pops her head out.

My heart is racing, blood thumping through my veins. My knuckles are gripping to the side of my Bonneville for dear life. The notebook and pen have fallen to the ground.

Bree is smiling innocently, like nothing happened.

"Noah," she says happily. "Come with me."

22

BREE

For some reason, Noah is splayed against his motorcycle looking like a deer caught in the headlights. His knuckles are white, clenched onto the sides of the bike. His blue eyes flash.

Then, something clicks. He looks angry.

"What do you think you're doing?" He explodes, brushing off his shirt. Storm clouds gather on his face. "Do you have a death wish for me or something? You've almost hit me with your car twice now!"

"Twice?"

"Don't you remember almost hitting someone one night in Edendale? On a pedestrian crosswalk?"

The night of the mediocre storm. "Wow, I'm sorry, Noah. I didn't realize—"

"Clearly." He glares at me, his voice dripping with sarcasm. "Might be worth actually watching the road when you drive. Just a heads up."

He runs his fingers through his hair. He's kind of cute when he's mad. I can't hold back my smile any longer.

Without any ability to stop it, my face breaks into a beaming grin.

He stares at me incredulously. "What is going on? Why are you smiling?!"

"I got a rise out of you." I know that I shouldn't feel gratified, but I really do.

"You're psychotic."

I roll my eyes, shrugging it off. I've heard worse. "Get in."

"Into the death trap? Absolutely not."

He stalks off down the parking lot. I put my car into gear and follow him slowly.

"Come on!" I yell through the window, honking my horn in time to his footsteps.

"Stop, you'll wake up the guests!"

"You know you want to." I blare music loud, whooping and hollering. "Please?"

"You're a menace."

"Pretty please?" I rev the engine.

It stalls. Silence.

I turn the key in the ignition once, twice. Then, I hear a very perceptible snort.

"That's what you get." Noah laughs as he steps onto the gravel pathway back to the Inn.

Okay, time for the last hail mary. I have no clue whether this will work. It worked when we were kids, but Noah and I have grown up since then.

"I found a storm!"

He freezes. Then turns slowly to face me, considering my words.

"Come on, it's close," I say, filled with a strange sense of desperation.

The pen and notebook are loose in his fingers and his

brow is furrowed. Then, a look of resignation crosses his face. "Can't. Up early tomorrow to bake for the guests."

But, he doesn't move so I try again.

"Are you sure?" My voice is calm, like I'm approaching a wild animal. "It should be a good one. I checked online. It's going to be big."

Below the steering wheel, I cross my fingers. Chasing storms has been a solitary activity for me in the last few years. But, maybe because Delia was so angry this evening, or because of my own anger towards my parents, I want nothing more than company tonight.

I want what we had when we were kids. I want *his* company.

He turns towards the Inn.

My heart stops. I scramble to think of something else to say, but I can't think of anything. This is it, he's leaving. For some inexplicable reason, I suddenly want to cry. I really wanted us to chase a storm together. What a stupid idea.

But, Noah doesn't walk away. Instead, he turns back around to face me. "One condition."

Anything. "Yes?"

"I'm driving."

23

NOAH

I click into the driver's seat and Bree settles into the passenger seat. A nervous excitement flows through me. It's been years since I chased a storm, and my options tonight were either to storm chase or stare at a blank sheet of paper for hours.

I frown, pausing with my hands on the steering wheel. For years, my life has been a clear-cut recipe — I help people and I'm there when they need me. I'm there for Dad, my sisters, Fernando, Colman's and Spruce Tree. I'm the opposite of Bree, who flings herself into life with wild abandon. She makes everything feel possible and exciting.

Maybe, just for one night, I can try things her way.

I turn the key in the ignition, bringing the car to life.

"How short are you?" I ask incredulously as I move the seat backwards.

"None of your business." Bree flips her braids. "You sure you can handle Garth?"

I shift into reverse. "Garth and I will be best friends in no time."

The engine stalls.

"Fine." I restart the car. "We'll be friendly acquaintances for now."

I gun the gas until the car purrs happily. Bree changes the dials on the radio, finally settling on NWR.

I grin. "I remember we used to fall asleep to this station when we were kids. Weirdest thing ever."

"It's not that weird," Bree says, a hint of defensiveness in her voice. She opens her phone and does some quick searching, going into navigation mode.

As I turn onto the road, the low humming of the car is comforting. The tension drops from my shoulders and I rest my arm on the center console. It's quiet, aside from the murmuring on the NWR station. It feels good to drive on a dark highway towards the promise of lightning. Bree sits back and we roll through the darkness together.

"How's your dad?" Bree asks. She used to love spending time with our family at Legacy. While we've caught up on a few things lately, we've carefully skirted topics relating to our parents.

"Good," I say, thinking of my ever-smiling dad. He rarely shows his sadness or anger anymore. "He's always good."

Bree looks out the window.

"What about your parents?" I venture tentatively.

Her smile drops off her face and her expression closes up.

I hope I didn't go too far — her parents have always been a touchy subject. When we were kids, she used to complain about them, and eventually, she flat-out refused to talk about them.

"Always good," she says, the words clipped.

"I'm your oldest friend," I say with a half-smile, remembering her words to me. "I don't believe that for a second."

She chuckles darkly and stares out the window. "Well,

they're in Europe so I should say they're doing fantastic. Apparently, leaving me behind to teach me to be 'responsible' is all they needed to be one big, happy family."

Her words are biting but there's sadness beneath the anger, making me want to reach out and grab her hand.

"Anyway," she says quickly, changing the subject. "You owe me a secret now. What is it that you're writing about?"

I press my lips together to keep the words in, but my heart softens a little. She did just tell me about her parents, I guess I could offer something in return.

"Someday, I'd like to write a book about the past," I say softly, almost hoping she didn't hear.

"The past — your past?" Her tone is soft as spring rain.

"Yeah," I venture and then add, "about Mom and my childhood."

And there it is, the topic I've struggled with for years. I've been wanting to write about Mom and my childhood since she got sick. I want to write about the love my parents had for each other — that one-of-a-kind, once-in-a-lifetime love that's as rare as ball lightning. And, in some cases, just as fleeting.

After she died, I had so many words, so much to say, so much I was feeling, but I couldn't get the words on paper. I couldn't even think about expressing how I was feeling out loud. Instead, I've been carrying it around for three years like a secret shame.

Until now. Of all people, why did I tell Bree? The words just came out. My heart beats loudly as I wait for her response.

"That's amazing." She reaches through the darkness and rests her hand on my wrist, brushing gently with her thumb. "If anyone can do it, Noah, it's you."

My shoulders relax, but I'm all too aware of the warmth of her hand. It's a very comfortable, almost intimate gesture.

"You always knew what you wanted." There's a smile in her voice. "There's no reason to hold back from getting it."

Her words fall over me like a warm blanket. The silence in the car feels safe and comforting. She pulls her hand away from my wrist, and I almost want to reach out and take it back. But, this time, not for her. For me.

A flash of lightning cuts across the sky.

"Eek!" Bree claps her hands and my stomach twists in excitement. In the distance, a boom of thunder. We're getting close to the storm.

Raindrops dot the windshield. The view becomes blurred as the rain falls harder.

I press on the lever to turn on the windshield wipers. Instead, I accidentally kick the car into cruise control. Panicking, I press on the other lever and the right turn signal comes on.

Bree laughs. "Aren't you supposed to be best friends with Garth by now? What are you trying to do?"

"Wipers." I press another lever. The hazards flash on and off.

"Need some help?" Bree asks through a fit of laughter.

"Never." Come on, Garth. One more try. I twist the lever and the high beams slash through the night.

Bree just about dies of laughter as the hazards, high beams, and turn signal work in unison. "This your first time driving, Sawyer?" She reaches over to twist the lever on the far right.

The wipers sweep across the windshield.

"I don't think Garth wants to be friends yet," I say, exasperated.

"Don't you blame my baby." Bree wipes a tear from her eye. "Pull off onto the side road up here."

I do, then shift into park and turn off the car.

A torrential sheet of rain falls down on us. The once-silent space echoes with the sound of rain and thunder. Lightning strikes and Bree's expression of wonderment matches my own.

Adrenaline pumps through me. I can't remember the last time I did something so exciting. Another shock of thunder rumbles the car.

Bree grabs a camera from the backseat and snaps shots of the lightning streaking across the sky. It's like we're kids again, wild and free.

"Hey." Bree has to yell over the rain hammering the roof. "Remember the game we used to play?"

My smile grows wider. Of course I remember.

"Scary stories during a thunderstorm," I murmur, watching the sky break open.

She laughs with excitement, lightning flashing in her eyes. She's beautiful, her face open, sincere, real. She doesn't hold anything back.

My heart thumps hard in my chest, and this time, I'm not sure if the storm is to blame.

BREE

*T*he sky is magic and I'm captivated. It's in the rain falling on the roof, the boom of thunder, the flashes of light. It's in the loud silence of the car. Usually, I play my audiobooks when sitting in a storm like this. But tonight, with Noah, I don't need them.

The rushing wind makes Garth rock on his suspension. The rain pounds the roof and I almost want to sing or dance with it. I don't know if Noah would find that weird — he never seems to mind my bizarre antics. I wonder whether he'll tell me a scary story, but the sound of the storm is enough for me.

Eventually, the time between the beams of lightning and the crashes of thunder begins to lengthen. The storm rolls away, further along the National Park.

Noah's leaning forward on the steering wheel, watching the scene. The lightning strikes and his face is lit in a momentary glow. He's watching with child-like wonderment, his eyes wide open. I've never noticed how beautiful his eyelashes are — thick and black. He has the slightest amount of scruff, highlighting his sculpted jawline.

We've been quiet for a while, but we don't need to talk. The storm must have lasted over an hour, but it feels like no time has passed.

Noah looks at me and I realize I'm staring. His clear blue eyes are piercing, stunning.

I take a deep breath and look away. I fumble with my seatbelt, clipping it in. "We should head back. Don't want my irresponsibility to rub off on you too much."

I don't know why I said that. I can't control my words when I'm with Noah.

He starts the ignition. "I wouldn't call you irresponsible."

"No?" My voice is bitter. "Then what would you call me?"

He considers my question for a moment and bites his lip. "Free."

Free?

Noah pulls a U-turn and we head back towards the Inn. His hand rests on the center console.

What would it be like to take his hand, to interlace my fingers with his? "You wouldn't believe what happened tonight."

I tell him the saga with the double booked room. I describe in blistering detail Delia's disappointment, how upset the Sharps were, and my luck with the kind bride who gave up the suite.

"And that's why Delia shouldn't trust me." I finish, shrugging.

Why did I tell him that? He probably doesn't care. Uncomfortable, I brood in the silence that follows. Then, to my utter surprise, Noah chuckles.

"Wow." He sounds... impressed? "You managed to get a rise out of Delia. DELIA. She's like the most mild-mannered, happy person on the entire planet."

I stare at him blankly.

He grins back. "Productive day for you. You got a rise out of both me *and* Delia. Well done. That's an accomplishment. We should give you a medal."

He does his half-smile and my tense expression relaxes. Leave it to Noah to turn a devastating situation into a small win. I stare out the passenger window at the darkness. The rain has stopped. I feel weirdly vulnerable all of a sudden.

"Well, what do you think about all this — about me working at the Inn?" My voice is quiet.

Silence from his end of the car. My mind is spinning.

"I think," he finally says, his tone matching mine, "you should lay off Delia. She's stressed about the summer, especially with all of the events at the Inn. Might be worth going easy on her."

"Hm." I frown at my reflection.

"Besides, maybe you'll like the work more than you expect." I hear the smile in his voice. "Maybe you'll get really, really, good at it. Picture this: Bree Lewis, Productivity Guru."

I roll my eyes. "My mom would be thrilled."

He laughs and we fall back into a comfortable silence.

Eventually, the lights of the Inn appear in the distance, signaling the end of our night. Noah's words stick in my mind. Delia's had every reason to give up on me and send me back to Edendale, but she's refused. And I can't imagine leaving her with her mile-long to-do list. I'm in too deep.

In a way, I actually admire Delia. With her skydiving and cowboy hats and frog figurine, she clearly owns her individuality, her "wild streak." Maybe at one time, she was irresponsible and careless like me.

Noah parks in the staff lot — without stalling, turning on the high beams, or going into cruise control.

We sit quietly as he turns off the car. He opens his mouth to say something, then stops himself.

"What is it?" I ask.

"Nothing," he says. "Just... thanks for this."

"For what?"

He shrugs. "I don't know. It's... I don't know how to explain it."

"Then don't."

He looks at me. "Don't?"

"Life's meant to be lived, not explained."

He raises his eyebrows. "And that means...?"

I laugh. "I read it in a book somewhere. I thought it sounded clever."

He unbuckles his seat belt. "It was clever."

I hop out of the car and take in Legacy Inn. A familiar feeling of determination washes over me. But this time, the motivation isn't destructive or self-sabotaging. I want to try my hand at being... helpful.

Noah gets out and stretches, throwing me the keys. He shoots me a charming smile, the kind that makes the girls at school go crazy. "See you tomorrow?"

"Absolutely." I fumble with the keys. My legs feel weak. It's nothing, I'm sure. It's just late and I'm tired.

Before we part ways, I face him once more. "Next time, you owe me a scary story."

25

BREE

*D*elia whirls into reception and goes straight to her office. I get up from my desk and pat down my skirt, taking a deep breath before following her. "Delia, can I speak with you, please?"

It's been a few days since Noah and I chased the storm and I've had a lot of time to think, replaying that evening in my head. I've stopped slacking at work — I arrive on time, take my designated breaks, and dress semi-professionally. Most of all, I try to stay on top of things. It's been going well. Delia happily answers my questions and there haven't been any more big incidents.

Most surprising, I don't despise the work. But I would never tell Noah that.

Today, I'm doing the unthinkable. Well, unthinkable for the old "careless" Bree — I'm asking for *more* responsibility. I steel myself and knock on the doorframe of Delia's office. She's sitting behind her desk, covered in tulle, satin and lace.

"Yes?" She raises her head, and a bit of tulle bounces with the movement.

I take a breath to calm my nerves, remembering Noah's words. I use the memory to propel me forward. "I know you're busy with everything around the Inn."

Delia takes off her half-moon glasses, waiting patiently for me to go on.

Why is this so hard to say? My hands are sweaty. "I was thinking... What if I help plan some of the events and weddings? I heard that we have a lot this summer, so, if you'd like, I could give it a go..."

I trail off, my voice small and quiet. This is a dumb idea. Delia's going to say no. Why would she trust me with such a big task?

But, to my surprise, Delia's face lights up.

"That is a phenomenal idea!" Delia leaps from her desk, rushes to me, and puts her hands on my shoulders. "I think you're well-suited for something like this. Event coordination was one of my first jobs, you know. That would be a big help, dear. Thank you."

I smile. It's not my "Customer Service" smile. It's a warm, genuine smile that matches the way I feel. "I'm happy to help."

My heart sings as I return to my desk. My mind fills with ideas and inspiration for the summer's events, so I pull out a pen and start making notes. Time disappears. The next time I check my phone, it's fifteen minutes past when I should have taken my break.

I skip to the kitchen, buzzing with excitement as I think about telling Noah. Since the evening we went storm chasing, we've been getting closer. That was the most fun I've had in a long time. Spending time with him is refreshing, like a cool shower on a hot day.

"Nooooahhhhh," I sing as I slam open the door. "Did you hear the news?"

"News?" Noah closes the fridge door. Fernando and Carrie have gone suspiciously quiet.

I bump my hip against his. "You're looking at Legacy's new Event Coordinator."

"Are you kidding?" He smiles, his eyes sparkling.

"Thought I'd put myself out there. Try to do a little more. The idea came highly recommended to me by someone smart." I wink.

"Yes," Noah agrees, "someone very, very smart."

I bite my lip. "Maybe not as smart as he thinks."

"Fantastico!" Fernando interrupts us, bounding over. "Noah, I'm sure Bree could use help with the catering side of things. Why don't you two team up for the summer?"

Fernando's voice is pure and sweet, but I don't trust his innocent gaze. Carrie gives him an elbow in the side, confirming my suspicions.

I roll my eyes and giggle. Their teasing isn't new. For some reason, these two think that there's something more to me and Noah. But we're just friends. Obviously. I wouldn't dare jeopardize his promising future.

"What do you say, partner?" Noah's eyes are full of laughter.

"Only if you provide me with an endless supply of fruit roll-ups."

He sighs like my request is an inconvenience. "Deal."

I give him a fist-bump. "Ready to go?"

"His shift was over *hours* ago!" Fernando exclaims dramatically. "Please, take him!"

26

NOAH

"*S*top!" Bree yells and I slam on the brakes. Garth rumbles to a stop in the middle of the highway — empty, thankfully.

My heart races and panic floods my voice. "What?"

But instead of appearing afraid or horrified, Bree smiles innocently. "Just thought this was a good spot."

We're on the border of the National Park and the storm clouds are gathering in the distance. I'd give us fifteen minutes before the storm hits, but for now, the sky is clear and colorful for sunset.

"Park here, and let's go for a walk." She turns off NWR.

"Aye, aye captain."

We're in a beautiful valley between mountain ranges, the sunset colors of the sky reflected in the river. A cool breeze swoops through the valley, forecasting the storm that's about to hit. The world is bright and the air is heavy with the impending rainfall. The smell of pine is intoxicating.

While I'm taking in the gorgeous view, Bree takes off up a small hill next to the road, her sandals almost flying off her feet.

"Where are you going?"

She pauses long enough to spin around. "Only one way to find out!"

I reach for boulders with my hands, scrambling up the hill right after her. We reach the top and Bree raises her arms in victory. The storm is coming quickly now, the sky dimming.

I flop on the ground and she sits next to me. To the left, the sky is yellow, orange, red. The sun sets behind a break in the mountains and the trees glow lime green in the light. To the right, the mountain peaks are covered with a blue and purple cloud.

And then, a flash of lightning. It's almost here.

"You scared?" she asks quietly.

"Never." My voice is husky, almost as low as the thunder.

The clouds rush in, angry and bruised, and we watch in silence. Within moments, it's clear that we won't make it back to Garth in time to stay dry. The first raindrop falls on my cheek.

I smile and take a breath.

Here it comes.

The rain falls on us like a bucket of cool water. Lightning flashes bright above our heads and Bree shrieks. She hugs her knees and tilts backwards, watching the lightning cut across the sky.

I sit back on my hands and Bree shifts closer, cuddling into my side.

Then, something inexplicable happens. Bree starts to giggle, and then it becomes a chuckle. Finally, she breaks into a massive fit of laughter, curled into a ball.

"Are you okay?" I'm mesmerized.

"I'm great!" She shouts, elated, and the thunder booms. "You should try it!"

I stare at her incredulously. She's lost it. "Try what?"

"Shout!"

"No way." My words vanish behind a clap of thunder.

"Trust me!"

She opens her mouth and screams into the chaos of the storm. Her voice is lost in the noise of the thunder and the force of the rain. But, as she yells into the darkness, I sense the release — the freedom.

Her eyes are wild. Her lips are pulled back in a beaming smile and her cheeks are red. She nods towards the scene ahead of us — the dark blue clouds, the flash of lightning, the sheets of rain and the trees almost blown sideways by the wind. It's an invitation.

I take a deep breath, meeting her eyes. I'm nervous and uncertain — I've never done anything like this before. But there are a few things I've done differently since hanging out with Bree. Her turquoise eyes sparkle and I decide to break from the recipe once again.

I shut my eyes, open my mouth and shout into the howling wind. The sound is, at first, tentative, and then loud. Louder than anything else. It goes on and on and I'm not even aware of my inhalations. My voice is wild and chaotic, and never in my life have I felt this free.

An image of Mom floats through my mind and, for once, I hold her there. I allow the grief to take over, and then be released into the storm. I abandon my guard and let memories of my childhood shine through. I feel it all — the loss, the sadness, the despair, the fear, the anger, the confusion. I let it course through me and disappear into the thunderstorm.

My lungs ache and my chest feels hollow. For once, I'm not the guy who helps everyone — the brother, the son, the friend, the student at Edendale High, the employee. I'm just Noah. And I've never felt so alive.

I shout until my voice is gone and I'm screaming silently to the wind. When I finally come back to myself, I'm aware that a small hand is wrapped in mine.

Confused, I look at Bree and she has an unreadable expression on her face. Like sadness, but relief. Happiness, but grief. My eyes meet hers and she gives me a small smile. Then, she throws her arms around me and squeezes me tight. The moment takes over and I squeeze her back, bringing her close. We're soaking wet, but I can't feel anything except the warmth of her body.

I have no idea how long we sit, wrapped in each others' arms. My eyes are clamped shut and I treasure the emptiness of my mind. Except for Mom. I'm holding her in the forefront and she's smiling. I'm overwhelmed by emotions that I've been pushing down and ignoring for far too long.

When I open my eyes, the storm is gone and the sky is dark. Night is upon us.

"Thanks," I whisper.

"Anytime." She sits back, looking into my eyes. "I think you needed that."

I'm lost in her gaze. The air around us is charged with electricity, and I wonder whether the storm left static behind. I feel like I'm seeing her for the first time, like I'm seeing everything for the first time.

My eyes drop to her lips. I'd really like to kiss her.

No, Noah, that's crazy. We're just friends.

"Ready?" I whisper, pushing away the thought.

She smiles and I stand, my wet clothes clinging to my body. I hold my hand out and help her up, but my fingers linger over hers. Something big just happened. Something I can't explain.

Then, she drops her hand and turns away, and the moment's lost.

27

BREE

*N*oah and I walk back to Garth, careful not to step on any wet grass or rocks. I can still feel his arms wrapped around me, burning like a sweet fire. Part of me wants desperately to grab his hand, but I cross my arms instead, trying to keep from shivering.

Watching him shout into the storm was one of the most powerful, beautiful things I've ever seen. In the end, I screamed with him — for my parents and my sister and my future and my present. At that moment, it's like he wasn't Noah and I wasn't Bree. We were just two people trying to figure out our ways in this world.

He sits in the driver's seat and slicks back his soaking hair. His white T-shirt is soaked through and his black slacks are stuck to his muscular legs. His eyes meet mine and I get lost in them.

Then, he smiles. My legs go numb and I look away quickly. Just the cold... Right?

We drive towards Legacy Inn, blasting the heat. My heart rate slows and a deep sense of calm flows through me. I'm lost in thought, some confusing, long-forgotten emotions bubble beneath the surface.

Over the years, I've gotten used to feeling alone, to being the odd one out. At Edendale High, all of my closest friends are part of cliques I don't belong to, nor want to belong to. However, tonight, with Noah, I had a glimpse of what it feels like to belong. With him, I allowed myself to be vulnerable in a way I've never been with anyone else.

It's comforting and yet unsettling.

"So, aside from screaming into storms like a banshee," Noah breaks the silence. "What do you want to do when you grow up?"

I shrug. "I do think the banshee thing is a promising avenue for me."

"Solid side hustle," he laughs.

I gaze out the window as my sadness and self-doubt threaten to return. I watch the stars appear — little pockets of light in an otherwise dark and empty skyscape. "Move to Paris, probably."

"Why?"

"To piss off my parents."

Noah laughs. "Your dedication to driving people crazy is legendary."

I smile at my soaked reflection in the window. Man, I am a sight for sore eyes. "At the start of the year, my parents were upset when I decided to take French instead of AP Economics. I started joking that I wanted to move to Paris after graduation and never return. The entire year, I went out of my way to research Parisian attractions, eat French food, and speak French whenever my parents were around."

I sneak a glance at Noah and he chuckles quietly, waiting for me to go on. I haven't told anyone about this — not even

Isla. "At the end of this year, my highest grade was in French, with a special note from Mme. Chevalier that I was 'super geniale,' which I'm pretty sure translates to 'super genius.'"

Noah drums his fingers on the steering wheel. "So, France it is."

"Maybe, maybe not." It's completely dark outside, now. There are no other cars on the highway. It's like we're the only two people in the world. "In all honesty, I don't know what I want to do with my life. I've only ever been told what to do and then rebelled against it."

Silence from his end of the car. Then, he places his hand on the center console and his pinky brushes mine. Did he mean to do that?

"It's a start." His voice carries a smile.

I meet his gaze and his eyes are kind. I'm flooded with a sense of relief. Admitting to Noah this most terrifying fact — that I have no plans for my future — feels good. I take a breath and stare at the glow cast by the headlights.

For the first time in a very long time, I want to believe that everything will be okay.

*A*nd everything does seem to be okay... almost suspiciously so. A couple of weeks later, I wake up excited to get to work. I hop out of bed and throw on a sundress, whipping my hair into a messy bun. I do a twirl in front of the antique mirror I found in storage and then assess my home.

I've made the loft my own in recent days. The creaky double bed is as comfortable as ever with my pillows and blankets, and fairy lights hang along the ceiling for the evenings. My clothes are folded in the dresser drawers, except for one drawer that I can't unstick for the life of me. All of my books and movies are stacked on the bookshelf. And just like when I was a kid, the loft is my favorite place to hang out — aside from the kitchen.

I bound down the stairs and into the kitchen, saying good morning to Fernando and Carrie — Noah isn't scheduled to work until later. I swipe a blueberry muffin and proceed to the staff room for breakfast. I grab two coffees before spinning into reception.

"Morning, Delia!" I holler.

"Is it?" Delia asks from my desk. She's got her face in her hands, staring at the computer screen blankly.

"Did you not sleep last night?"

"I did. Here."

I hand her one of the coffees. "What can I do?"

"The Jordan wedding is this weekend and the weather is looking terrible. I asked them to have a back-up plan for bad weather, but they never responded. I was too swamped to follow-up with them and now the worst has happened." Delia sits back in the chair, defeated.

I frown and come around the desk. "Let me see if I can help."

Delia chugs her coffee and I study the screen, puzzling things together. My stomach flips in nervous anticipation. This is the first real wedding/event issue I've had to deal with since I've been training with Delia. While I think I have the concepts down, I haven't had to confront a problem. The pressure to get it right is overwhelming.

Here goes nothing.

"Okay," I say slowly, trying to overcome my nerves. "The Jordans were specific about having the ceremony outside. What if we have it in the gazebo, with a tent set up just beyond for the attendees? It's a small ceremony and I think we could fit the guests in there. And, for the reception, we can have it in the events room, as we do with indoor weddings."

Delia stares at the screen and pushes her glasses further up her face. "We've never done that before."

I wait with bated breath, my heart racing. It's a stupid idea.

She abruptly stands up from my desk and the chair almost falls over. "That's fantastic! Thank you, my dear. I spent hours working on that. I wanted to set something up in the garden or near the docks like we normally do, but this is much better."

She grabs my face and kisses both cheeks. "Well done, Bree."

A blush spreads across my face and I clear my throat as an answer. I'm not used to being fawned over.

"Anytime," I say, hiding my smile with the rim of my coffee cup.

29

NOAH

"Noah! Let's go!" Bree's melodic voice carries over the song on the radio. She pops her head into the kitchen and stares at me impatiently.

Carrie and Fernando look up from the closing checklist, taking in Bree's disembodied head.

"Well, go on!" Fernando booms. "Bree is waiting for you. It's time for your date!"

Bree and I roll our eyes in tandem. He will never let this go. "It's not a date!"

"Oh, excuse my English," Fernando says unconvincingly. He thinks he's so funny. "It's time for your 'hang out.'" He adds the air quotes with his fingers.

I sigh. "Don't you guys need help closing up?"

Carrie peers at me over her glasses, her hands on her hips. "Noah, your shift is over. Don't make me grab a dishcloth and swat at you."

Bree sticks her hand around the door and taps at an imaginary watch. She's been hanging around the kitchen so often lately, it's hard to believe she doesn't officially work with us. On her breaks, she often chops vegetables, helps prepare dessert for the guests, or cleans the counters — all the while singing loudly with Fernando. There've been a couple more dance parties in the kitchen and Carrie's even joined in, but I'm happier spectating.

It's hard to believe it's been three weeks that we've been at Legacy Inn. Bree has totally stepped up her game — she shows up on time, troubleshoots guest issues, and actually seems to care about her job. The extra help is very much appreciated around the kitchen and Fernando and Carrie are completely enamored with her.

On top of that, Delia has been training Bree and I on the events for the summer, and it's clear that Bree is a natural. She's full of new and creative ideas for decorating and planning, while I'm happy to take the catering side of things. I can't say I know much about furniture placement and lace and frilly stuff — to the disappointment of my sisters.

"So, where are we headed now?" I ask as we cross the staff parking lot. It's a warm, calm evening, but it won't be that way for long.

"I could tell you. Or I could let the suspense build." Bree grins. "Guess which option I'm going to pick?"

"Fine. But I'm still driving."

She rolls her eyes and tosses the keys.

I click into the driver's seat and start the car. I'm excited. There's electricity in the air, and it isn't just from the upcoming storm.

Bree bounces in her seat and bites her lip while adjusting the dial on her portable radio.

She might be my favorite person on the entire planet.

30

BREE

"Okay, this is serious." Noah frowns towards the dark horizon, his voice stern. We're parked on the side of the road, waiting for the storm to hit. "Power of flight or invisibility?"

I furrow my brows like I'm thinking hard and then relax into a smile. "Flight. Obviously."

"Obviously?"

"Don't tell me you're one of those people obsessed with invisibility?"

"Do you know me at all?" He laughs. "I'm pretty much invisible already."

"You're a lot of things, but I'd never call you invisible," I say. The girls at Edendale High linger by the parking lot to see him drive up on his motorcycle, wearing his cool leather jacket. He might be a loner, but people take notice.

"Why not? I'm pretty proud of my most distinguishing characteristic." He winks at me.

Does he really not know?

"You're gorgeous," I blurt. Oops. My face turns bright red

and I stare out the window. Ohmygosh. "Not like... you know. Like the girls at school fall over themselves for you. How can you not notice that?"

Noah looks genuinely confused. "I never paid much attention. None of the girls at school really interested me."

"No?" I ask, and my heart speeds up for some reason. "Not even Isabella Hall?"

Noah bursts into laughter. "Wow, you've got my type pegged."

"She's hot!"

"Sure." He shrugs. "But, I never had... chemistry with her. Don't get me wrong, I can see why guys fall for her. But she never made me feel anything real. You know?"

Noah looks at me and his piercing blue eyes carry an indecipherable message.

My heart picks up speed again and my breath catches. I clear my throat, looking at the horizon. "Yeah. Of course."

I must be catching a cold or something. My face feels warm and my heart is racing. I'm acutely aware of Noah's arm, resting next to mine on the console. He's Noah Sawyer, Edendale High's mystery dreamboat. He's practically famous and he doesn't even realize it.

And what was I expecting — that he would say something about me being special? I'm not. I'm just Bree, his childhood friend.

"So, if you had the power of flight," Noah asks with a smile, "you'd fly straight to Paris?"

"I'm not sure Paris is first on my list," I say, happy for the subject change. "I want to go places with epic storms, like the midwest, Florida, the Carolinas. And then, someday, Venezuela, the Congo. Maybe I'd do it for a year. Travel to the most insane storm locations."

Noah has a cryptic smile on his face. "A year of storm chasing."

A thrill passes through me. Something about it feels so right. "Exactly."

I've never considered storm chasing as a possibility in my future. Though I'm not sure I could do it forever — there's far too much driving involved — I never would've thought to follow this hobby of mine for a year. My options have always seemed very cut and dry — either go to school or get lost in the world. Speaking to Noah, I feel for the first time that there might be a third option.

As though the sky applauds my choice, the first flash of lightning appears in the distance. I stow away the map on my lap and the portable radio. Within moments, the flashes double, triple above our heads. The thunder booms and the sound of rain on the roof energizes me.

I watch, captivated by the show. For every storm I've chased, there's always something different — the sound of the rain, the pattern of the lightning, the boom of the thunder. Each storm is individual, like a snowflake or a fingerprint.

Imagine. Following storms for a whole year. Eating greasy cheeseburgers at truckstop diners. Staying in cheap motels and checking maps by lamplight. Tracking lightning, and hail, and maybe even tornados. That's a future I can look forward to.

"You owe me something," I say quietly.

"What's that?" Noah's leaning over the steering wheel, watching the storm.

"A scary story."

Noah grins. He places his arm on the center console so it's almost touching mine again. Before I can think about it, I link my arm through his — like when we were kids. His eyes meet mine for a second and I can't keep the smile off my face. Everything about this moment is perfect. Noah has to be one of the most amazing people I've ever met.

Then, with his body warm next to mine and the storm raging all around us, he takes a breath to tell a story.

31

NOAH

*B*y the time I finish the scary story, Bree is wrapped around my arm, her fingernails digging into my skin. As I spoke, the story took on a life of its own — a haunting tale about a ghost and a secret tomb.

Silence fills the car. Goosebumps creep over my skin and the nerves take over. Did she like it? Was the story good?

"That was," she says, her voice low. My stomach drops as I wait for the verdict. "Incredible!

I laugh, my cheeks burning.

"Haunting," she says. "Like scary but not gory. Thrilling but not horrifying. How did you come up with that?"

"Thanks," I say. "It was loosely based on real life events."

"WHAT?" Bree looks appalled.

"Yeah. You know the ghost that hides in the tomb?"

"Yeah..."

"I based it off this girl who hid in the fridge and pretended she was a raccoon."

Bree shoots back in her seat and punches me lightly in the arm. Part of me wishes she hadn't let go. The storm is passing now, the rain pattering lightly on the windshield.

Bree stares out the window, her mind clearly elsewhere. Hearing her say that she enjoyed the story feels like the highest praise.

I turn the key in the ignition and start the car.

"Have you thought of writing mysteries or thrillers?" Bree asks as we turn onto the highway. "That improvised story was miles ahead of many thrillers I've read or listened to."

"Not really, I've been so focused on writing about Mom." Then, a half-smile crosses my face. "Someday, though, I'd like to write thrillers."

"I would buy every one of your books," Bree says, her voice sincere. "As long as they're not all based on me."

Too soon, I'm parking Garth in the staff lot. Self-conscious, I place my hands in my lap.. I can't stop thinking about when Bree was wrapped around my arm when I was telling the scary story.

Just like when we were kids. Right?

She stares out the windshield, looking troubled.

Before I get the chance to ask her what she's thinking, she opens the passenger door and jumps out.

Time to move on.

"Night, Noah." She gives me a salute and a wink. She stops in the parking lot and I stand in front of her.

I have an overwhelming urge to stay with her, to take her hand, to do something. Her eyes meet mine and I get the briefest sense that she might not want to leave either.

No, don't be crazy, Noah. Don't forget where you come from.

"Night, Bree," I say instead, forcing a bright tone.

She punches me lightly on the arm and then walks to the Inn.

I stare after her, making sure she gets in okay. When the door shuts behind her, I head down the gravel path.

Then, something strange happens.

With every step, it's like I'm walking through a barrier. A yellow light appears in my mind, like a weak, flickering candle. I pick up speed, walking quickly through whatever is standing in my way. The candle grows brighter and brighter.

I break into a run.

I reach my cabin, drop my bag and rip the notebook and pen from the top drawer of my dresser. I sit down at the desk and I put pen to paper. The words flow like water. A weight lifts with every scratch of the pen.

I write about Bree, mostly. I write about our childhood, our adventures, the excitement I felt to see her every summer. And, like a tap left open, I write about my family — my sisters, Dad, what it was like growing up in a loving home.

And finally, I write about Mom, her sickness, her space in the world. Our world.

I write until my hand hurts and my eyes sting from exhaustion. When my words run out, my face hits the paper and sleep carries me into a peaceful dream.

32

BREE

"Well, dear," Delia stands in the doorway to her office. "I think it's time we call it a night!"

I put down the portable radio I'm currently frowning at. It stopped working today — must be out of batteries. "You sure?"

"Absolutely. You've been doing great work lately." She smiles, then heads back into her office.

Is this how it feels to be respected? To be taken seriously? I grin. It's hard to believe that I've been at Legacy for a month now. I've enjoyed my time more than I could've imagined. The Legacy staff feel like family and planning the events has been one of the best parts of my days. Every issue that pops up is a puzzle to solve, and there's a never ending series of challenges for me to work out.

I glance at the portable radio and sigh. No storm chasing tonight, though it's probably for the best. Noah and I have been chasing storms at every opportunity. At first, we only hung out for that reason, but now, we find any excuse to spend a couple of hours together after our shifts. We've taken to watching scary movies in the staff room and listening to audiobooks together.

It's a bit unnerving how much I enjoy talking to him. I feel like I can tell him everything about myself and he just listens. He never forces me to speak, nor does he sit uncomfortably in silence. He offers advice when I ask for it, and otherwise, he asks intelligent questions that encourage me to think deeply. Unlike many people in my life, he never assumes that I'm up to no good.

The most surprising thing about him, though, is that I never tire of him. Sometimes, I feel like we could spend days together and I'd be happy every minute. Must have something to do with how close we were as kids.

"Why don't you wrap up and head to bed?" I call after checking the computer one last time. "I'll finish up a few things and shut the reception right afterwards."

"Whatever you'd prefer," Delia says gratefully from her office. Moments later, she emerges with bundles of red and polka dot fabric in her arms. "Good night, Bree. I'll see you in the morning."

I finish the last of the to-do's for the evening and lock the reception, taking note of the time. It's probably too late to hang out with Noah, but before I climb the stairs to the loft, I pop my head into the kitchen to say good night anyway. The kitchen is bright, but empty, and the radio is off. I guess everyone left.

Feeling strangely disappointed, I head up to the loft and change into my PJs. I've got a scary movie loaded up — something about a ghost in the attic — and, with my snacks at the ready, I press play.

I'll admit, the movie makes me nervous, given that I'm alone... In an attic. Part of me really misses Isla.

The ghost is materializing into physical form, about to

attack an unsuspecting woman, when a massive strike of lightning flashes through the room.

I shriek and instinctively dive under the blanket. A moment passes and I laugh and inch the blanket back off my face.

A storm? This is fantastic!

The thunder claps overhead and rain explodes onto the roof.

Then, another crack of lightning. Everything goes black.

The lights along the ceiling are out, the fan whirs to a stop, my computer battery light is extinguished. Goosebumps erupt over my skin. I suddenly don't love this.

But minutes go by and the power is still out. I sit in the darkness, unable to shut my eyes. Should I do something? Should I flip the breaker — or whatever it is that dads always talk about in movies and TV shows?

After a few more minutes, I decide that I need to get out of bed. I might as well try and find the breaker thing. Plus, pitch darkness gives me the heebie-jeebies.

I tiptoe across the floor and look down the dark staircase. The hair on the back of my neck stands. Scenes from scary movies and thrillers flash before my eyes. I always shout at the stupid girl on the TV screen about to enter the dark staircase — *Don't do it!*

And now, here I am, doing it.

I take one step down and the world swims before my eyes.

Two steps down.

The darkness reaches its claws out to grab me, pull me under.

No, don't be silly Bree. This isn't a movie.

I tiptoe down the rest of the stairs, letting out the smallest shriek. I plead with all of the gods not to send a monster to eat me. I make it to the bottom of the stairs unscathed and jiggle the door handle desperately.

My hands shaking, the door finally bursts open. I'm about to walk into the event room when I become aware of a dark form just ahead of me. The form has a rectangle head and long arms.

Delia?

No, too tall to be Delia. Fernando?

No, too slim to be Fernando. What is that thing?

My mind is flooded with possibilities — An alien? A vampire? A werewolf?

No. It must be human. But if it's human, what's with the square head? Unless... it's a ghost.

My heart stops. I might collapse from fear. I'm frozen on the spot, begging my legs to run back upstairs where it's safe. But before I can flee, the thing — whatever it is — sees me.

It reaches out and I feel a cold, dead weight on my arm.

This is it. It's taking me.

My survival instinct kicks in and I scream.

NOAH

I close the fridge door just as a boom of thunder shakes the building. Strange, I would've expected Bree to come knocking if there was a storm tonight. Maybe she's got something else going on.

A flash of lightning slices the sky and the power goes out. I'm left in the blackness of the kitchen.

Good timing. I just finished stocking up the vegetables in the fridge — my last chore of the evening.

I head over to the lone window and gaze at the dark world outside. The aggressive tap of raindrops on the windowpane is almost deafening. Another flash of lightning and the world comes alive. Trees sway in the wind, puddles form in the parking lot, and thunder rumbles from the heart of the sky.

It would be a great night to be storm watching. I wonder if Bree is enjoying it.

I take off my apron but keep my hat — I'll use it going back to the cabin. I'd love to chase storms with Bree tonight but returning to my notebook is a nice consolation prize.

I've been writing consistently since I first told Bree that scary story. It's like the floodgates have opened.

With a smile, I pop my hand in the fridge to be sure it's running on backup generators, and then head out into the event room. It's cloaked in darkness and I stand for a moment to let my eyes adjust.

Behind me, I hear a creaking noise. My heart speeds up. Could it be one of the guests? Carrie? Fernando, maybe?

I turn to face whoever it is that's behind me. I open my mouth to say hi when a flash reveals that it's just Bree.

Then, I put my hand on her arm.

She screams. The sound rips through the air, disturbing the silence and piercing my eardrums.

"Bree, woah!" I whisper-shout, shaking her arm. "It's just me!"

"You?" Her voice is strangled.

"Noah!"

Now that my eyes have adjusted, I can see her blink in the darkness. She's white as a sheet. I remove my chef's hat and hold it in front of me.

"What's wrong with your hand?" She squeezes my hand, feeling for my fingers. It's like she's inspecting me to make sure I'm human.

The tension flows out of me and I laugh. "I had it in the fridge a second ago. Sorry if it's cold."

"Frozen, you ghoul!"

I laugh again and finally take in what she's wearing — a big shirt that says "Bee Kind" and short shorts underneath. I snap my head up to look at her face. She does have nice legs, though.

"Anyway," I say awkwardly, running my fingers through my hair. I was *not* checking her out, I wouldn't. "Big storm, hey? I'm going to head to the cabin. The rain sounds so nice on the roof. But I guess the rain sounds nice wherever you are..."

I'm blabbering, willing myself to stop talking. Now that I can see her, I can't get over how cute she looks. Her hair is tied up in a bun, her face looks like an angel's, and she's got the most perplexed expression. I just want to put my arms around her.

What? Noah, no.

"So yeah," I finish awkwardly. "See you tomorrow."

I salute her, turn on my heel and head towards the exit of the event room. I trip on a chair almost immediately.

Wow, fantastic exit. Not awkward at all.

"Noah?" Bree's voice is small. She hasn't moved from her position at the bottom of the stairs. Her hands are clasped together in front of her.

"This sounds stupid. But, I was watching a scary movie alone in the loft and the stairs freak me out and the power's out and it's just..." She takes a deep breath. "I'm scared."

I cock my head to the side. When we were kids, she used to get scared at night. Her parents wouldn't let her have a night light, so I asked my mom for one, then gave it to Bree to use in the loft.

She takes another breath and releases her hands. It looks like she's trying to take a casual, confident stance. "Would you mind sleeping in the loft with me? There's space on the floor so we wouldn't share a bed or anything. And of course you can say no! It's just that the movie is about a ghost in an attic and it's just me up there and I'm kinda freaked out."

She hiccups a laugh. "*And* I almost just got beheaded by a ghoul with frozen hands."

I chuckle, unsure what to say.

In my silence, her face falls for a fraction of a second.

Bree always tried to play the brave and strong one, the girl who protected her sister. Even though it's been years since we spent any real time together, I know who she is. I can tell by the small wrinkle in her brow, by the slight turn of her smile — she's scared. I can't leave her alone.

"Okay," I say tentatively and her face lights up. "I'll sleep on the floor."

"I might have a pillow or two you can borrow. But..."

"But?"

"Fair warning — there's rumors of a raccoon in the loft."

I snort. "I'll take my chances."

Our footsteps rumble up the staircase, frightening away any ghosts that might find themselves in the loft.

34

BREE

I arrive at the top of the staircase and bound over to the bed.

Noah follows, stripping off his hoodie and tossing it to the floor.

Maybe it's weird that Noah and I are sharing the loft, but we used to sleep here all the time as kids — even sharing the same bed. Things might be different now, but one thing hasn't changed: I still need protection from ghosts.

I throw him a pillow and smile shyly. When was the last time I had a sleepover? And when was the last time I had a sleepover with a *guy?* It was probably Noah, years ago, in this very loft. It shouldn't be weird, though — we've done this a million times.

So why is my heart racing, even now as my breath returns from darting up the stairs?

"Want another?" I ask.

"Nah, the floor is more comfortable than expected."

I laugh, staring at the ceiling. Flashes of lightning streak through the window. Now, without the threat of ghosts, the sound of rain on the roof is soothing.

Minutes go by and my heart rate slows to a regular pace. I feel safe here. I'm at home in a way that I haven't felt in a long time. It's the way I wanted to feel — hoped to feel — with my parents if we managed to work things out in Europe.

Family, warmth, safety, home. These are luxuries I never felt I had.

Lying in the darkness with Noah, it feels like we're in a dream of summers past. "My parents hated that I would come to them when I was scared at night. Remember the—"

"Nightlight?"

"Yes! The cartoon lion." I smile. That lion got me through so many spooky nights. "Leonardo."

Noah is quiet for a long time, and I wonder whether he's fallen asleep. Maybe it's better if he has.

I pull my blanket up to my neck. "I remember dealing with everything alone — my fear, my anger, my anxieties. It was hard. As Isla got older, I knew I needed to be the safe space for her. I needed to be home for her." I take a deep breath. Once again, I'm saying too much, but Noah does this to me. I've never let myself acknowledge or vocalize these thoughts.

"It's been my priority for as long as I can remember — be there for her because that's what I wanted the most." I take a shaky breath. Noah's probably sleeping. Who cares to hear the truth if the truth isn't important? "But the only reason I knew how to be there for her is because of you and your family. You were home to me. Whether you were keeping me safe from ghosts or giving me a night light for when you weren't around."

You *are* home to me. The realization leaves me breathless because I haven't let myself feel it. I clamp my mouth shut before I can utter the words. I can't burst into his world and jeopardize his promising life. I'm a sinking ship and I won't take him down with me.

The rain falls on the roof like classical music and my heart thumps to the beat. Only one thing could have allowed for this. Right here, I'm home.

35

NOAH

*B*ree's words echo through my mind as the rain patters on the roof. When I'm with Bree, I could believe that we aren't on Earth anymore. We're in a dream, some magical place made for the two of us.

Her confession about her family breaks my heart but doesn't surprise me. It's comforting to know that my family was home to her. My parents were poor, but never poor in love.

"When you made me shout into the storm, I thought you were crazy," I say, breaking the quiet. "When you made me tell you a scary story with thunder all around, I thought you were clinically insane."

"We still haven't proved I'm not," Bree says, a hint of laughter in her voice.

"Or maybe you're the normal one," I say. "Since spending time with you, I can write again. You were my childhood and because of you, I can write about what it was like, and what Mom was like. I can remember her, and everything feels... okay. Because of you, the memories feel bright and wonderful. I can't thank you enough for that."

Silence stretches between us and I look up towards the bed, wishing I could see her face.

Bree shifts on her bed, the springs groaning beneath her. "You know what I don't understand? How do you have time for it all? You balance school, work, taking care of your family, and now, writing a book. How do you do it?"

"Caffeine."

"I've literally never seen you drink coffee."

I laugh. Then, a sobering reality hits me and I take a deep breath. "My top priority is *always* to help others, to support everyone. Anything for me comes second."

Bree is quiet. Speaking honestly like this is refreshing — like drinking lemonade on a blistering hot day.

"After Mom died, Dad's carpentry business was struggling. Even at thirteen, I knew that we couldn't survive on one income and Mom's hospital stays and treatments ate up most of our savings. So, I started asking for jobs. It was never a question for me. Now, it's up to me and Dad to support our family. The things I do for me have to come second." I feel the grief of lost time, lost opportunity. So much is lost when the world only sees you one way. Writing could never be a priority for me and I used to feel incredible guilt doing it. But Bree makes me want to try, to dream big for the first time in years.

"My parents say love is overrated." Bree's voice is cold. "Love is for the people that advance you to the next step of success."

I want to take her hand. I can't imagine growing up in an environment that doesn't believe in love.

"The truth is, I've lost my belief in love. Not for others, of course, but for myself. My house doesn't feel like home and my friends in Edendale are temporary. I don't belong anywhere."

I keep my lips pressed together to stop from saying the one thing I want to say: you belong with me. But the truth is I have nothing to offer her. And she knows it. There's a reason we stopped being friends three years ago.

"Date after date they've forced me into," she says, exasperated. "And now, they've set me up with this Andrew Stewart guy. Apparently, he'll help me run the Inn one day." Her voice is robotic, a cold, distant front. The words aren't her own. "Merging together Legacy Inn and Stewart Aviation is the best way to grow our business."

36

BREE

I'm thankful for the sound of the rain on the roof as, otherwise, you could hear a pin drop. In the silence, the blandness of my life hangs like a white cotton sheet. There's my future. Graduate high school, go to an Ivy League university, run the Inn, marry Andrew Stewart, have 2.5 babies and die of functional alcoholism at the reasonable age of eighty-two.

Boring.

Unable to stop it this time, my mind swirls into a mess of emotions. Rage for the strict rules my parents have given me, desperation to be anything but what they say, and then an aching desire for something resembling love.

Through the chaos in my mind, I barely hear Noah's next words. "You don't have to let them define you."

Everything stops. Goes quiet. I'm listening now.

"Whether you're rebelling against or following their rules," he says, "you're still making a decision based on them. But you don't have to let their wishes choose for you."

The meaning behind his words hits home, and a sob

threatens to escape my throat. He's right. I've been letting my parents choose for me, guide me, define me. For every choice I make, every decision I consider, my parents are at the forefront of my mind. Will they like this or dislike it? What will they say? Will they finally pay attention?

The chaos disappears and I'm left with a profound feeling of sadness. More than ever, I wish Noah and I were laying on the bed together, just like when we were kids.

"What happened to us?" I whisper, my voice raw.

Back then, I had a reason. My mom didn't want me rubbing off on the responsible Noah Sawyer. The "great kid." I knew the downfall that awaited him if he spent too much time with me. My mom drilled it into me. But why did he let me go?

I rack my brain to remember something, anything.

When Noah speaks, his voice is forcibly light. "Three years ago, I asked you on a date."

What?

"I asked you to the meadow, the one we always used to go to, and I wanted to tell you that I felt something more for you."

My heart has officially stopped in my chest and I dare not breathe.

"I hoped that you knew that it was a date. When I showed up to your house, I was wearing a suit and I brought you flowers, like Mom told me to." He cracks his knuckles.

I hear the smile in his voice. I don't remember any of this.

"I got to the front door and I was about to ring the bell when I heard your voice. You were talking to your mom. I heard her say that I was a great kid, responsible, all that. And then, your response. That we were 'just friends and would never be anything more than that.'"

My stomach drops. I did say that. I was hurt because of the "great kid" comment and I wanted her to stop speaking.

Noah chuckles awkwardly. "I suspected that you staged the exchange on purpose to let me down easily. I took the hint and started pulling away. When I didn't hear from you again, I assumed that you didn't even want to be friends anymore. And then, Mom died and everything fell apart."

My throat is dry but my stomach is flip-flopping. No. How can I tell him that I never would've done such a thing?

"I completely understand why." His words are rushed.

I'm frozen, a statue. I can't even blink.

He shifts and the floorboards creak beneath him. "I never meant to push past our friendship or anything. And, you know, that was all in the past. Those feelings have disappeared, I want to assure you of that."

My heart cracks, just a little. Back then, I tried so, so hard to push my feelings down and keep my hopes at bay. But, of course, I hoped it was a date. I was crazy about him.

Was?

My heart beats loudly and I finally let myself acknowledge my feelings for Noah — feelings that are more than friendship. Have I always had these feelings for him? He's my be-all, end-all — the first person I think about in the morning and the last person I think of before bed. Since we met, not a day has gone by that I haven't thought about him.

But, I can't bring him down with me. I'll only ever bring him trouble and pain. Sadness threatens to consume me and tear me in half. Now that I know what I feel for him, I want to scream it from the rooftops, or whisper it in the dark. I want nothing more than to believe I can be with him.

With a sigh, I turn on my side and see his face. He's laying on his back and his eyes are closed, looking like the perfect still portrait. Never in my life have I felt so vulnerable. I want to reach out and grab his hand.

I want to believe in love... with him.

37

NOAH

*M*y heart races. It's tough to breathe.

There it is, the reason that we stopped being friends — all because of my embarrassing gesture. The amount of times I wanted to call her or pull her aside to talk to her, but I couldn't do it. And then, Mom died and my mind was preoccupied, even though I wanted to turn to her the most.

I never told her my feelings for her, obviously. Now, I worry. Did I go too far? Did I say too much?

The rain stops.

The silence feels so loud.

"I remember that day," Bree says. She moves to the edge of the bed, looking down at me. "My mom was going on about how I was too reckless and too flighty. She brought you up, said you were a 'great kid' to imply that I wasn't."

My brow furrows. I didn't hear that part of the conversation.

She continues. "I felt selfish, I didn't want to bring you down with me. I had a feeling that it was a date, but I insisted we were just friends. I didn't want her to know that I wanted to date you too. The lecture she would have given me..."

I almost choke. She felt the same way?

In the darkness, my eyes meet hers. I can see everything on her face. Her future. Her past. Her hopes, fears, and pain.

I gaze at her face and all of my doubts and fears leave. I always believed I was never good enough for her, but now, I know that I'd do anything to make her happy. I want to reach out, touch her, grab her hand, hug her. Anything to be close to her. For the first time in a long time, I let myself be real with my feelings for her.

The truth is, my crush never went away. I'm in the heart of the storm crazy for Bree. I would trust her with my life. She's the most breathtaking person I've ever known.

My eyes linger on her lips and her breath catches.

She starts to lean in and I lean in too.

But then, her face contorts. Some unreadable emotion flits across her eyes and she pulls away. She rolls onto her back, her walls up again.

"That's it for me tonight," she says. She's got the mask back on. "Night, Noah."

I lay back on the floor. I wanted to kiss her. I wanted to show her how much she means to me.

"Night." I close my eyes and let images of our childhood flash behind my eyelids. Jumping off the dock together, building forts in the forest, baking cookies in the Inn kitchen with Mom. Happy memories of a time I'd repressed.

Then, a soft hand finds mine in the darkness.

Bree's arm hangs off the side of the bed. She intertwines her fingers with mine, clasping my hand tight.

When sleep finally takes me, her hand is still wrapped

around mine and I'm rubbing my thumb along her fingers, the movement lulling us to a place almost as beautiful as reality.

38

BREE

*S*unlight beams through the window. A cool, fresh light — the kind you get after a good storm. My hand is wrapped in Noah's, resting on his chest. His chest rises and falls with each breath, and I briefly allow myself to wonder what it would be like if my head was resting on his chest, my arm looped around his waist.

I don't want to move, I don't want to wake him up.

Even in sleep he has his trademark smile.

What's he dreaming about? Maybe about last night? I can't believe everything that we talked about. It feels like something out of a movie.

My lips tingle as I think about how I almost kissed him. Man, did I want to. But at the last moment, the memory of my mom's voice berated me and I pulled back. All I could hear were her stern words, telling me to stay away from him.

I could kiss him to piss her off, or I could hold back to follow her rules. But it's like Noah said — if I'm doing something to rebel or follow her rules, I'm still doing it for her.

What do *I* want, without factoring in my mom, dad, or

anyone else? My mind kicks up all kinds of scenarios, all sorts of options.

I squeeze my eyes shut.

What do I want? Not "what does Mom want for me." Not "what do I want to rebel against." What do I actually want?

An image immediately pops in my head. I'm standing in the rain with Noah, his arms around me, my lips on his. That's what I want. I want to kiss Noah. It's the first thing I've wanted for myself in a long time.

I just hope he'll try again.

I shift so I'm closer to him. He looks like a happy, sleeping puppy. But cuter. Finally, I see what I never let myself see before. The abrupt angle of his jawline and of his chiseled cheekbones. His square nose and his long, black eyelashes. He's one of the most beautiful people I've ever laid eyes on.

His hair is getting long again. It's lush and thick and I want to run my fingers through it. Maybe I can do it now, before he wakes up. Without thinking twice, I lift my hand tentatively. Noah continues snuffling and I reach forward.

Almost there.

I touch a strand.

And then his eyes shoot open.

"AH!" I shriek, flying backwards and toppling sideways off the other side of the bed.

"You trying to kill me again?" Noah booms and then sits up.

Willing my cheeks to stop burning, I pop my head over the bed. "I thought I saw a bug."

Noah looks around suspiciously. "A bug?"

"A spider," I say. It's not my best lie. "A big one."

"Where is it now?"

"It was just a piece of hair." I scramble to stand. "But. For the record. You should be thanking me. Not a lot of girls would try to save you from a spider."

"Uh huh. Sure."

I dance around the bed and hold a hand out to help him up. "You mean: thank you."

He stands and flattens his shirt. "My hero."

"And don't you forget it." My false bravado disappears when I remember I'm wearing tiny pajama shorts.

Fortunately, Noah is keeping his eyes on my face. He takes a step closer so we're almost face to face. Well, my face to his chest.

Is this when he kisses me?

I tilt my face up and soften my expression.

Rather than taking the obvious sign, he steps around me.

I almost fall face first.

"You have the day off too?" He looks out the window. "I have an idea."

"Yerg?" I mumble.

He bursts into laughter. "Get dressed and meet me downstairs. I want to take you somewhere. If you'll come?"

His crystal eyes are dancing and my throat goes dry. Of course I'll go! But, my mouth refuses to work. I nod, dumbly, like one of those nodding dogs you see on people's dashboards.

Where is he taking me? Why are my legs weak again? And why, oh why, do I want nothing more than to kiss him?

39

BREE

*B*ut it seems a kiss will have to wait.

Noah disappears down the staircase and I spin around the room, letting out a little squeal. Last night was unreal. Now that I'm finally acknowledging my feelings for Noah, I can't wait to see him again — this time on a date.

I stop spinning and frown at my reflection in the mirror. It is a date, right?

Or did I get it all wrong? Maybe I've assumed that he likes me, but that isn't the case anymore. He did say his feelings were long gone... Maybe I've completely blown this up in my head.

I search for something appropriate to wear. I want to dress casual in case we're just going as friends, but I also want to wear something cute in case it *is* a date.

I rifle through the dresser drawers and pick out the perfect outfit — a cute sundress with sunflowers. I tie my hair into a half-ponytail and then, to play up the casualness, I add my favorite pair of white converse. Good enough.

"No matter what happens," I murmur to myself, "I'm doing this for me."

With a final twirl in front of the mirror, I skip down the stairs.

Noah waits for me at the bottom. He's wearing a black t-shirt that hugs the muscles of his chest and his black hair is shaggy. His eyes light up. "You look beautiful, Bree."

"Thanks," I stammer, blushing.

"Come on." He takes my hand and pulls me towards the kitchen.

Fernando and Carrie bustle about, singing and whistling, respectively, to a rock song.

"Change of soundtrack today?" I ask.

Fernando looks over impassively. "Carrie won our latest bet — that the power at the Inn would go out before August."

Carrie pumps her hand and Noah gives her a high-five.

Right, there was a power outage. With everything else that happened last night, I'd almost forgotten what brought Noah and I together.

Noah plops a picnic basket on the kitchen counter. With a cryptic smile, he says, "Take anything you like."

"Is that so, amico?" Fernando shakes his finger at Noah. "Because of you, we are almost out of food!"

Noah bursts into laughter and swings open the fridge. "Maybe out of cheese, Fer, but that isn't my doing."

They continue with their bickering while we stock up the picnic basket for breakfast and lunch. By the time we latch the picnic basket, my sides hurt from laughing.

"Uno momento!" Fernando exclaims. He unwraps a plate of colorful cupcakes. "Please, take some."

"I don't think they'll fit," Noah says, eyeing the over-stuffed picnic basket.

"Silence, no more arguing," Fernando's smile betrays his

serious tone. He plucks a couple of cupcakes from the plate and places them in a takeout box. "For your date."

Instead of protesting, Noah and I look at each other. It's the moment of truth. My heart beats fast in my chest and my stomach fills with butterflies yet again.

He glances down at our clasped hands and then gives me his trademark half-smile. A warm feeling washes over me and I smile back.

Noah grins. "For our date."

It's official.

I'm on a date with Noah Sawyer.

40

BREE

I've never experienced cloud nine but I'd imagine it feels a lot like this. My hand in Noah's, we race to Garth in the staff lot. I click into the passenger seat and Noah smiles at me again, his eyes sparkling with mystery. Where is he taking me?

We pull away from the Inn. I take his hand, our fingers comfortably intertwined, and he kisses the top of our clasped hands. My heart skips a beat.

We drive towards Edendale, chatting happily about our past. I've got the window down and the air smells like pine trees. The gentle purring of the car is comforting. Eventually, Noah signals and turns onto a gravel road.

I stare out the window. This is familiar. But why? When did I come here?

Then I remember. It's the same gravel road that I turned onto the day that I almost skipped out on Legacy Inn. I remember stopping next to that grassy space to answer Delia's text. Here, I decided to go to the Inn, but only to drop off chocolate milk. How could I have known that choosing to stay at Legacy would be one of the best decisions I'll ever make?

My body buzzes with electricity and I squeeze Noah's hand, grateful for each and every choice that brought me to this moment. We continue down the gravel road and my mind is flooded with happy memories of our summer together.

Noah stops the car. It's a nondescript area with thick forests of trees on either side of the road and gravel reaching to the horizon behind and ahead of us. There really isn't much to see.

"Is this it?" I ask hesitantly.

"You'll see." Noah smiles and hops out of the car, his eyes twinkling. He grabs the picnic basket and holds out his hand. "You coming?"

I weigh the pros and cons. Con: I have no clue where we are or where we're going. Con: we could get murdered out here in the dense Montana forest. Con: that's a lot of branches and brambles for a girl in a sundress and white Converse.

Pro: Noah is reaching out to me with a playful look in his eyes and I trust him to take me anywhere.

With a smile, I grab his hand and let him lead me through the forest. Soon, we pop out of the bushes and I'm about to make a joke about him murdering me when I catch sight of the view.

We're on the edge of a large meadow. The grass is green and bright, like the sun is shining from beneath, and wildflowers throw shades of every color across the field. Directly ahead, the peaks of the National Park glow white in the morning sun and, on the far side, a gathering of cliffs overhang into the meadow. A summer breeze brings the scent of fir trees and pollen. The sound of chirping birds and rustling leaves makes me feel completely at peace.

I know this place. Distant memories return to me. I've been here before, many times. It's a long-lost treasure from my past.

We came here often when I was a kid — me, Noah and his family. We used to run through the meadow, eat fresh bread on a picnic blanket by the cliffs, and watch the sunset color the peaks. We used to play games, talk, dance and dream here.

"Noah," I whisper in awe. "Thank you."

41

NOAH

I blink against the sunlight, enjoying the cool breeze flowing over us. I don't think I'll ever stop smiling. It's afternoon and I can hardly believe how the time has passed. With Bree, time is elastic. It's a construct, not constricting. I normally want to rush to the next thing, but with her, I never want our time to end.

We spent the last few hours the way we spend all of our time together — laughing, talking, teasing, joking. We chased each other through the meadow, ate a delicious lunch in the wildflowers, and even tried to climb the cliffs.

Now, we're lying on the blanket staring at the sky. Bree's head rests on my arm, her legs intertwined with mine. I hold her hand on my chest. Her hair smells like coconut shampoo.

"It's coming," she says, a thrill in her voice.

The sky is turning darker by the minute. She wiggles closer to me.

"Trying to steal my heat or something?"

"Something," she says innocently.

I laugh. "Did you know that a storm was coming today?"

"The NWR said something might be passing through this evening," she says. "But I guess it is almost evening."

The sky is getting angrier and we should probably move, but there's not a single part of me that wants to disrupt this moment. The winds pick up and the first rain drops dot my face.

I assess the distance to the cliffs. We're near enough that lightning shouldn't be a risk. Then, the thunder booms and the sky breaks open. A mountain lake is released onto us and I burst into laughter while Bree scrambles to her feet.

"Come on!" She darts towards the cliffs.

I pick up the soaking blanket and run after her.

We stand under the cliff overhang, watching the world change around us. The trees lining the meadow move with the wind. The rain creates waves in the grass and wildflowers. The lightning and thunder roll in the clouds above us.

We're the only still images in this wild portrait. But not for long.

Over the weeks that Bree and I have been hanging out, she's allowed me to see a side of myself I haven't seen in a long time. She makes me want to try new things and have fun. Her spontaneity constantly inspires me. Anytime I feel stressed or anxious, all it takes is a look from her, a conversation with her, to calm my nerves.

And right now, there's just one thing I want to do. I grab her hands, smiling devilishly at her. Even with her hair soaking wet and her sundress wrinkled, she's still the most stunning person I've ever seen.

"What're you doing?" she asks.

Slowly, I step back from under the cover of the overhang, taking her with me. I bring her into the rain and she laughs.

"Dance with me," I say with a shy smile, pulling her close.

She brushes a strand of hair out of my eyes and steps closer. Without breaking eye contact, I wrap my arms around her and take her hand. There's no need for music — we sway with the beat of the rainstorm. The thunder and lightning crash above our heads but it's just us in this perfect moment, and the force of the rainstorm urges us forward.

42

BREE

*M*y heart races and I'm barely aware that I'm soaking wet. I'm pressed up against Noah, swaying to the melody of the raindrops. Somehow, without any music, we're keeping time together, like we're listening to a song no one else can hear.

Never in my life have I felt so alive — so awake, excited, happy and safe. How is it that Noah makes me feel at once wild and free, but also completely at home? I thought this was a thing of fairy tales, not real life.

I hug him close, allowing his arms to circle tight around me. My hands are clasped behind his neck and I hope I never have to let go. The last three years we spent apart feels like a dark, bland memory. If the timeline of our lives was made into a painting, that time was grey compared to the wild colors we had when we were kids, and now again since I've been at Legacy Inn.

The reality of my feelings for him floods my entire body and my stomach fills with butterflies. I feel his heartbeat and I know he's as blown away as I am by this magical moment.

Maybe now's the perfect time for him to kiss me.

As though he knows what I'm thinking, Noah begins to slow. He leans back to gently look into my eyes and my breath catches. The world goes quiet and my thoughts disappear.

In slow motion, he brings one of his hands to my face. He sweeps the hair from my eyes and cradles the back of my head.

I look at his beautiful lips.

He leans in and I stand on my tip-toes.

Then, a flash of lightning sparks behind my eyelids and his lips meet mine. The world stops spinning, the rain stops falling, time stops ticking.

It's just Noah and I in the eye of the world's most dazzling storm, and I know that he'll never let me go.

43

NOAH

*T*he next three weeks are a blur of stolen kisses, quiet confessions, and rolling storms. On rainy nights, I sleep in the loft and we fall asleep with our fingers intertwined. During breaks, Bree comes in the kitchen and helps us with various tasks before starting impromptu dance parties. I join in, and I even get Fernando to teach me a few spins and dips to use on Bree. During the rare moments where Bree and I aren't together, I scribble away at my book, finishing two to three pages a day.

Will we be this happy when summer is over? I try to tell myself that there's no point in worrying. We have to live in the moment.

"Ready?" I ask one evening as I enter the reception.

Bree looks up in surprise and then shoots me a beaming smile.

I want to grab her hand, spin her, and kiss her, but Delia has politely warned us about being too "friendly" in front of the guests.

"Just about—"

"Bree," Delia calls from her office. "Would you be a dear and bring me the stapler?"

Bree skips into Delia's office with the stapler and I follow close behind. We're greeted by chaos. Though Delia's office has slowly improved since she started handing tasks off to Bree, it seems that today is an exception.

Bright red tulle and polka dot scarves are strewn around the room. There are paper lanterns and boxes of fairy lights spread across the ground. A feather boa adorns the aerial photo behind Delia's desk. The frog figurine has a tiny black hat.

"Can we help with anything?" Bree asks tentatively, assessing the sheer amount of fabric.

Delia looks up from the floor where she's sitting with her legs spread open, hand sewing red fabric with a scowl. "Oh, hello Noah. It's this darned roaring twenties party this weekend. If I could just get this table runner back together. I knew last year's Moulin Rouge party got out of hand, but how did *this* even happen?"

Delia holds up the table runner in frustration and I see the problem. There's an irregular hole directly in the center.

Almost instantly, Bree straightens next to me. "Maybe this can work to our advantage."

"How do you mean?" Delia asks, her irritation apparent.

Bree steps forward and grabs the fabric delicately.

I cross my arms and watch her in action. I have full trust in whatever she's got in mind.

"This'll go on the food table, right?" she says. "What if we place the cake on a cake stand in the middle of the hole—"

"So it looks like the cake is raised on a red velvet pedestal," Delia finishes the thought.

I half-smile while Delia stares at us through the hole.

Her face relaxes into a beaming grin. "Brilliant, Bree! Once again, your idea takes the cake. Oh ha!"

Delia bursts into booming laughter. My heart is full of pride as I watch Bree shyly tuck a strand of hair behind her ear. There's nothing in this world I wouldn't do for her smile. I can't imagine feeling for anyone else what I feel for her.

Bree signs out of work and grabs my hand, pulling me towards the staff lot.

"We have to hurry!" She smiles with a twinkle in her eye. "I have a surprise!"

"Can I get a hint?"

"It involves fruit roll-ups."

"That's not much of a surprise."

With Bree's directions, we make our way towards the National Park. The air is electric. I beg Bree to tell me what the surprise is but she keeps her mouth shut. We reach the edge of the storm and the rain falls in sheets. I expertly turn on the windshield wipers.

"You're getting good at that." She laughs.

"Practice makes perfect."

The first strike of lightning flashes. Thunder booms. We sit in silence, captivated by the scene. Each storm is different, beautiful in its own way. Experiencing them with Bree makes everything sweeter.

"Okay, ready?" Her expression is impish. She kicks off her shoes and dives into the backseat. She lowers the seats, revealing a stack of pillows and blankets, along with a box or two of fruit roll-ups. She lays out the blankets and grabs her computer from the pile, setting it up in the middle.

"Just like when we were kids." She pats the spot next to her self-consciously.

I lay next to her on the blankets. She sets the computer

in front of us and presses play. The title of a scary movie appears on the screen. Her face glows red with the color on the screen and I'm filled with a familiar feeling. Bree Lewis is the most amazing person I've ever met. When I'm with her, possibilities feel endless and the most mundane things feel exciting.

The truth is, I love her. I love everything about her — from her hilarious PJs, to her intelligence, to her dance moves. She inspires me every day, with a smile or a laugh or a wink.

A flash of lightning almost blinds me. Seconds later, a loud crash of thunder booms and Bree shrieks. The thunder goes on and on. When I open my eyes, Bree is curled against me, hugging her knees, and my arms are wrapped tight around her.

"If only a movie could scare me like that," she says, fear in her voice.

"Well, you know I'll always be here to protect you."

The words are a joke but they're actually true. Bree quiets and tilts her head to look at me. I gaze into her beautiful eyes, losing myself in them.

"I love you, Bree." There it is, plain and simple. "You're everything to me and you always have been. Even my mom knew it."

Bree cuddles further into me.

I kiss the top of her head. "You bring me to life, you make me want to do things I've only ever dreamed of doing. You've flipped my world right-side up and you've changed me forever. I can't imagine a day without you."

She runs her fingers through my hair. She does it often and the gesture is insanely comforting.

"You are something else," she whispers. "I didn't think people like you existed — especially for a girl like me. You're my home, Noah, you've always been my home. I love you, too."

Her voice breaks with the force of her smile. My heart might explode and I know, without a shadow of a doubt, that I will always love her. She brings her hand to the back of my neck and I lean in to kiss her. Our lips meet. This is the start of the rest of our lives.

BREE

"A severe weather warning is in effect in the County of Bonnyton, forty-five miles west of Edendale…"

I turn up the volume on my portable radio. That's not far from here. The automated voice describes the possibility of heavy rainfall, lighting and thunder.

In other words, my bread and butter. My stomach flip-flops in anticipation of seeing Noah when our shifts are over. It's another great night for a storm — whether we choose to leave the Inn on another road trip, or stay here and watch a horror movie in the loft. My favorite is when he tells me a scary story while the rain falls on the roof.

An elegant older woman sweeps into reception.

"Bonjour." She places her passport on the desk dramatically. "I would like to check in. Mme. Dubois."

"Let me help." I open the rooming list. The portable radio is blaring weather updates and I hastily turn it down. "Mme. Dubois, you're staying with us for a couple of weeks. Where are you visiting from?"

"Paris, of course."

I smile cordially. "I was thinking of going there."

Mme. Dubois purses her ruby red lips. "Whatever you do, don't come in the summer. Far too many tourists! You won't be able to appreciate the beauty of the city."

I laugh, choosing to ignore the fact that I would be one of those dreaded tourists. I swiftly finish checking her in and she leaves with a passing "adieu."

An uncomfortable feeling nags at me. I'd forgotten about the plan that I had just two months ago — live in Paris to piss off my parents. That was the future I saw for myself.

Since that time, it's like I've entered another life. At Legacy, I've discovered a new side of myself. I've grown and flourished on my own terms. The staff are close friends and I take ownership of my role and solve problems.

The reception runs like a dream and Delia's stress levels have decreased steadily as she's trusted me with more tasks. Coordinating the events and celebrations is my favorite part of the job. Whether it's placing paper butterflies on a baby shower banner, or a red bowtie on a quinceañera cake, adding a unique twist is one of my favorite things to do.

Aside from spending time with Noah. We've been together for a month and a half and, every day, I fall for him a little more. I've never felt so happy to be myself, to explore what I want to do and how I want to do it. His quiet, tentative nature brings me down to earth. For the first time, I understand how people can spend years with someone without getting bored.

I try to rid myself of the nagging feeling threatening to spoil my current happiness. I leave the mail in Delia's office and, on a whim, I check the Wall behind the door. The lovely pink cowboy hat sits untouched and unruffled. Delia has cycled through a few cowboy hats this summer, but I haven't seen her wear this one.

I return to my desk and turn up the volume on the radio.

"You lovely girl." Delia dances into reception carrying a bike helmet, a sandwich, and a lightbulb. "I ran into Mme Dubois and she raved on and *on* about you. I didn't know you could speak French!"

"Un petit peu." Delia stares at me with a confused expression on her face. I burst out laughing. "A little bit!"

"You have done exceptionally well this summer, my girl." She swoops into her office, her brown cowboy hat tipped backwards on her head and her green dress reminiscent of peacock feathers. She swoops back out again with her hands behind her back. "I think it's about time you were rewarded for your work."

With a flair, Delia whips her hands around. She holds my favorite pink cowboy hat.

"What?" I gurgle.

"This is for you!" She places the hat on my head. "I can't tell you how much I appreciate everything you've done. I know you have a bright and exciting future ahead of you, but should you ever choose to go into the Inn business, you have my vote."

I blush and give her a warm smile. For every time that my parents have ordered me to run the Inn one day, never have I truly considered it as a real possibility.

"I know I've said this a few times," Delia continues. "But you do remind me of myself. You've grown up so much this summer and have come so far. I know your parents would be proud."

Delia exudes warmth and kindness but my smile falters. The nagging feeling returns. Right, my parents. The two people I've ignored all summer. Isla and I have kept in contact so they know I'm alive, but that's the extent of our communications.

"Thank you." My voice is robotic.

Delia squeezes my hands and sets off, leaving the reception in a hurry. I stay where I am, letting the uncomfortable moment settle over me. In two weeks, I'll be back in Edendale, back at school, back at our house. I can't fight a very persistent, unappealing thought. If I make my parents proud, won't they forget about me?

I try to stand strong, but doubt consumes me. What am I doing here? Is any of this real? Is this truly who I am, or am I just acting out who I wish I could be?

I picture this pathetic caricature. A flighty, irresponsible girl of sixteen, standing alone in the reception of a mountain Inn wearing a frivolous pink cowboy hat. Playing pretend. Playing like she belongs.

The music changes on the radio.

No, let's not go there. It's fine, everything's fine.

I center the hat firmly on my head and sit at my desk. But the computer screen blurs.

What am I doing at Legacy Inn?

45

NOAH

*I*t's an unusually quiet afternoon and Fernando and Carrie let me go early. I hang up my apron, thinking of Bree. These past couple of months have been nothing short of amazing. I feel like we could spend forever together. She's my future, just like we've fit into each others' pasts.

For the first time in years, I'm making time for the things — and people — I love. I've written over half of my book. I write after our dates, before work, or in the loft while she's sleeping and a scary movie plays in the background. I have time when I'm with her.

I barge into reception, smiling.

Bree looks up in shock and her pink cowboy hat almost flies off.

"That's a great look!" I say.

She smiles and I can't look away. One glance from her can take me down.

"Thanks." Her voice is distant. Instead of signing out for the day, Bree remains at her desk, her brow furrowed.

"Ready to go?" I watch her face carefully.

She blinks a few times like she's been snapped out of a dream and shifts her papers around. If I didn't know better, I'd say it was a nervous tick, an avoidance technique.

But then, she looks at me and her expression brightens. "Let's do it!"

She gathers her things, chattering about her morning. I file away her strange behavior — I must've imagined it. She comes around the desk and I grab her hand, but it hangs limply in mine. I try to catch her eye, but she heads towards the door.

"Come on, Sawyer! We don't have all day."

We reach Garth and Bree carelessly tosses her cowboy hat into the backseat. I frown. Something is definitely off. The hat means everything to her and her throwing it away is definitely a red flag. We get on the road and silence falls between us. She stares out the window at the passing trees, her hands clasped in her lap.

"Everything okay?" I ask hesitantly.

"Of course!" Her voice is bright. Too bright.

"You can talk to me, you know."

"Always do."

But the car remains silent. We turn onto the gravel road and I park. Bree stares out the window without making any moves to open the door and I wait patiently, wondering if she'll open up.

She turns towards me and her eyes are guarded. "Do you think I'm too irresponsible?"

Her voice is careful, like she's been rehearsing the words in her head.

The question trips me up. I know my answer matters — a lot. What is it that she wants to hear? I opt for the truth.

"No," I say slowly, "I think you're exciting and carefree. I love that about you."

Her eyes go dark. Without a word, she turns back towards the window and my stomach twists into a knot.

I don't think that was the answer she was looking for.

46

NOAH

a rose detaches from the wreath, hitting me on the cheek. With a touch of frustration, I attempt to re-attach the flower. The thorns poke me viciously as I stick the tape around the stem. I pull my fingers away and I get a sliver from the exposed wood.

I glare at the wreath — what a piece of work.

It's a Saturday and I'm spending my shift in the games room, attaching flowers to a wreath for a wedding. But, I'm working with Bree, so I don't mind.

"This rose really *pricked* a fight," I say with a half-smile.

Bree isn't looking at me or at the rose that tried to decapitate me. She's staring determinedly at the flowers she's tying to the wreath, her face blank and her eyes unfocused.

The gnawing feeling in my stomach grows stronger. I've been trying all morning to get *some* reaction out of her.

When she asked me to help earlier, I couldn't say no. She looked so impassive, it was just another hint that something is bothering her. I was hoping to talk to her now, but she's distant.

Nath enters the room and drops another heaping basket of flowers on the table.

"Thanks, Nath." Bree mutters distractedly.

"Y'all had better use these flowers for good! They're my pride and joy."

"You better be-*leaf* it!" I quip. Not my best work.

While Nath gives me a light, sympathetic giggle, Bree continues working.

I hold back a sigh. For the past few days, her mind has been elsewhere. She rarely visits the kitchen, and Fernando and Carrie exchange worried looks when they think I'm not paying attention. I go to reception on my breaks to spend time with her, but she insists she's too busy and sends me away. On top of that, we haven't been storm chasing in days.

"I've heard that you two have been gallivanting all around the area," Nath says to me warmly as Bree works. At least I'm not the only one she's ignoring. "Have you any plans for the rest of your day?"

Nath's expression is friendly and open, but she shoots a worried glance towards Bree.

I force a smile. "We're headed to the meadow."

"The one towards Edendale? Your mom loved to bring you kids there."

"I remember," I say. "She used to make us sandwiches while we ran around the meadow and climbed the cliffs. I think she liked it there because we tired ourselves out."

Nath pats me on the shoulder. I don't mind talking about my mom anymore. It feels good to remember her.

"Both of you will be going... Bree?" Nath's question hangs in the air and we turn to Bree.

"Wha?" she mumbles, coming down to earth. "Yeah, yeah. The meadow."

With that eloquent answer, she returns to what she was

doing. Nath offers me a sad smile and places her hand on my shoulder.

"Talk to her. She feels safe with you," she whispers.

Nath leaves the room and my eyes travel over Bree's face while she continues to tape the stems. She's wearing jean shorts and a black top today, her hair in a cute bun. But there are dark circles under her eyes and a crease in her brow.

Something is bothering her and I want to find out what. But, I also know Bree. I can't push her too hard or I might lose her forever.

47

BREE

"The alternator's out." Noah wipes his hands on a cloth and tucks it into his back pocket before closing the hood. He leans forward on Garth and every arm muscle pops.

I give him a nod and try not to notice how insanely good he looks right now.

It's a hot afternoon, the kind of hot where you can watch heat waves rise off the asphalt and your skin burns in minutes. I'm excited to get to the meadow, but Garth isn't cooperating.

Noah takes off his cap and runs his fingers through his hair. "I can fix it if I get some time and enough tools. I'm sure Vin's got some lying around."

Of course he can fix Garth. Noah is perfect in each and every way.

While Noah cleans up, I brood in a downward spiral of doubt and uncertainty. Delia meant well with her words, but her mention of my parents has affected me. No matter how much I try, I can't shake the despair that wants to pull me under.

At night, I play scary movies or audiobooks to help me sleep. I'm grateful for the radio at reception because the music helps keep the thoughts at bay. And Noah is the best medicine. Or at least, he would be, if my dark thoughts didn't revolve around him.

While I'd like to believe that I've done something good this summer — I've helped Delia, Carrie, Fernando and Noah — I can't quell the aching fear that I'll let them down. Just like I've let my parents down. Given the messes that I create, Noah will be the first casualty. But how can I risk hurting someone that I love? Will Noah be left broken and hurt by me too?

I can't bear the thought. I want nothing more than to spend all of my minutes with him, but how can I do that if those minutes might end in pain?

I stare darkly over the parking lot. On top of all my worries about letting my Legacy family down, now I also have to figure out what to do with this alternator. As though he can read my mind, Noah takes my hands.

"It's going to be okay," he says. I hope he's right. I place my arms around his waist and pull him close. He leans down to kiss me.

When he pulls back, there's an unmistakable sparkle in his eyes. "I might have an alternative."

He takes my hand and drags me out of the car. We jog across the parking lot, coming to a stop in front of his motorcycle. "What do you think?"

My mouth goes dry looking at his Bonneville. "You want to take me on a motorcycle?"

"Only if you want to."

I wrap my arms around myself. I'm terrified by the prospect, but I've always dreamed of doing this. My mom would be so pissed. "I've never been on one."

"Don't worry. I won't let you get hurt." Noah's eyes twinkle.

"That's not what I'm worried about," I mumble. A cautious smile spreads across my lips. I reach up and brush his hair from his face.

I take a deep breath and some of the fear subsides. I'd trust Noah with my life. "Let's do it."

Noah places his spare helmet on my head and gives me a kiss before putting on his own. He gets on the bike and turns it on, revving the engine. Then, he instructs me to get on the back seat and tells me how to sit while we're riding.

"Hold on tight!" He shouts over the noise of the engine.

"Got you." I wrap my arms around him and lean into his back. He smells good, like soap and trees.

The rumble of the motorcycle is intoxicating and I feel a small tingle of excitement. Noah squeezes my thigh before gunning the engine. We peel out of the staff lot and head towards the highway.

We hit the road. It feels like we're flying. Adrenaline flowing through me, I lift one arm and cheer while cars zoom in the opposite direction. The air rushes over us and I'm breathless from the force of movement. I hold onto Noah tight, feeling his abs constrict in laughter.

The best part? My mind is blank of everything but the exhilaration of speeding through time on two wheels.

My arms get cold and I cuddle back into him. Happiness floods me and I rest against his back, allowing him to warm me up. Noah never ceases to surprise me. I tilt my face forward and my eyes linger on the horizon. I see his cute half-smile in the side-view mirror.

I squeeze my eyes shut and pray that this moment will never end.

48

NOAH

*B*ree wraps her arms around my midsection and my heart beats fast. It's been months since I rode my bike. It's even better being back on my Bonneville with Bree fitting perfectly behind me. I could almost forget that something is bothering her.

Almost.

All too soon, the ride is over. We approach the gravel road on the left and I guide us to a stop near the meadow.

"That was AMAZING! I loved it!" Bree shrieks and hops off the bike. She removes her helmet and, as soon as I've got mine off, she launches herself into my arms.

I kiss her. "Thought you would."

I grab our bag from the back compartment, then I take her hand and we walk through the meadow. It feels like we're back to how things were — back to the Bree and Noah we were just days ago. I let myself revel in it, hoping it never ends.

We lay out the picnic blanket and Bree shuts her eyes against the sunlight. I smile contentedly at this person I'm so deeply in love with and then flip open my notebook. I count the pages and discover that I'm almost at the end of my novel.

While Bree sprawls in the sun, I put pen to paper and let my words flow. I get lost in writing, but Bree and I don't need to speak. It's enough to know that she's here.

"Question for you," I ask. "What do you think about leaving the book open-ended?"

"Like with a cliff-hanger?"

I laugh. "If only my life was *that* exciting."

She snorts and then looks at me. "Well, life is open-ended."

A hint of sadness hides behind her eyes, but she turns away and closes them again.

I think about her words for a moment and then continue writing.

Bree takes a deep breath in. "Do you think I've 'grown up' this summer?"

She has that tone again — the forced casual question that somehow feels loaded.

I tense up. My answer matters a lot to her and, given that I let her down on the last question, I don't want to risk making the same mistake. How do I tell her that she's perfect as she is — that she doesn't need to change a thing about herself?

"You don't need to," I say, instead of something that actually makes sense. I curse my lack of smoothness.

"What do you mean?" Bree props herself up on her elbow.

"You don't need to grow up. I love you as you are. You can grow up, of course, if you choose." I scramble, slightly panicking. Why are my words coming out like this? There must be a better way to phrase my thoughts. "You're wild and free and exciting."

Bree's face clouds over and she flops onto her back.

My stomach twists. I said something wrong. Again.

"Too wild for the Stewarts, of course," she grumbles under her breath.

Her words land like a slap to the face and something inside me shifts. The Stewarts? Like Andrew Stewart — the guy that she had a date with at the end of August?

A chill travels down my spine. Her face is dark and troubled, and her arms are crossed over her chest. Is that what she's worried about — not being enough for Andrew Stewart?

I stare blankly at my notebook, my mouth suddenly dry. Why does Bree care what Andrew Stewart thinks of her?

49

BREE

*C*louds rush across the sky like they have somewhere to go. They appear, then disappear, one after another. Shapes forming, then breaking apart.

It's comforting, a reminder that I can't expect anything to stay the same forever. My heart hasn't slowed down since the bike ride. Maybe I had too much coffee. Or maybe, my dark thoughts have returned in full force. All I can think is that I'm too wild, too irresponsible — too this and too that, but still never enough.

Certainly, I'm too wild for Andrew Stewart, and for that, I'm endlessly thankful. But am I too irresponsible for the boy lying next to me? He says he loves that about me, but how can that be?

When I open my eyes, the sky has changed once again. An angry purple cloud hovers just out of my field of view. A storm is coming, it'll hit in about ten minutes. The storm cloud looks like a mushroom — this'll be a hefty one.

It creeps across the sky. The wind picks up and the trees rustle around us. We don't have much time.

"The storm looks big." Noah closes his notebook. "We should go."

"Not yet," I whisper, lying still and staring at the sky. My mom's voice echoes in my head, droning on about how reckless I am. I'll always be that way.

"Okay." Noah says, but he sits up and packs a few things.

The first lightning bolt streaks across the sky. I watch it without blinking.

"Seriously," Noah's voice is urgent. "Let's get out of here."

"It's not so bad." I clench my teeth together to stop from shivering. The goosebumps along my legs and arms betray me.

"You're cold. I have a tarp in my bike so we can cover ourselves before it hits."

"I'm not cold." My teeth click audibly together mid-sentence.

Noah smirks. "Liar."

An icy wind freezes me to the core, and the thunder booms. I can't take it a minute longer. Noah's right, I'm frozen.

"Fine." I feign exasperation and roll my eyes. "Let's go then."

I scramble to a stand and Noah folds the blanket.

The sky breaks open. The rain is violent, the lightning right above our heads. Thunder crashes and the world shakes. This storm isn't classical music or even rock. It's death metal.

A small piece of hail bounces off the top of my shoe.

Adrenaline shoots through me. If we stay out here, we'll be pelted. I look at Noah. "Run."

We sprint across the field. Just before we reach the tree-line, lightning strikes a tall pine. There's a loud crack, like a gunshot.

Hail sweeps across the meadow. It's still small, but getting larger. Running into the forest is a terrible idea, but staying in the open is a death sentence.

We dart into the forest and the rain and hail pound the canopy aggressively. We reach the gravel road but I can hardly see Noah's bike from the roadside. The rain falls in a grey sheet and the world has gone dark. I can't remember the last time I experienced a storm this intense.

"Wait here." Noah shouts. He hands me the blanket and disappears into the rain.

I set it out under a large pine tree and take a seat, wrapping my arms around my knees.

Noah emerges from the darkness with a bundle of fabric in his hand. Within moments, he sets up the tarp so it sits on the branches above us.

Hail tears through the forest canopy. Each piece is the size of a dime.

"Take these." Noah shoves his sweats and leather jacket into my chest. His jaw is tense, his teeth clenched.

"You need them," I manage through my shivers.

"You need them more."

He lays the jacket over my shoulders and leaves the sweats at my feet.

I wait a beat and then slip into the clothing. I wrap my arms around my legs once more and my shivers slow. Noah sits at the other end of the blanket and rests his arms on his knees. We watch the world dissolve outside our little fort.

The temperature drops.

And the hail gets larger.

It crashes around us like bullets. A chunk the size of a golf ball rips through our tarp, bringing the pooling water with it.

I cry out.

Noah pulls me to him and wraps himself around me. "It's okay. You're okay."

The world flashes and the sky roars. Chunks of hail crash through the canopy, branches cracking and snapping. The trees sway. The wind blows so hard that the hail is coming at us from the side, rather than from straight above.

I curl into Noah and close my eyes.

After what feels like twenty years, the violent sound of hail wanes, dissolves into the steady patter of rain. The storm passes.

I'm still wrapped in Noah's arms.

"Are you okay?" Noah checks my face, and then runs a hand over my hair and down my back.

I hiccup, still terrified beyond belief. "Ye-yeah."

Concern sparks in his blue eyes. He wipes a tear from my face. There's a cut on his cheek. It's shallow and bright red. Almost like he cut himself shaving.

"You're bleeding," I say.

"A piece of hail skimmed me. It's no big deal."

The piece of hail is still near his feet. It's almost the size of a tennis ball, and rough like sandpaper. It tore through the tarp like a butcher knife through butter, and if it had fallen an inch to the left...

I shiver. Not from the cold, but from fear. We stayed in the meadow too long because of me. We got trapped in the storm because of me. Noah was cut because of me.

And he was almost killed.

Because of me.

Noah holds me close and glances towards his bike. The seat is pummeled and split, the body of the bike is banged up, and the windshield is cracked. The side-view mirror I checked on the way here is broken, lying flat on the ground.

"It's just surface damage. We'll be able to get back to

Legacy and I can fix everything there." Noah nods to himself. "The important thing is that we're safe."

He's right. The important thing is that we're safe.

We got lucky.

If we'd listened to me...

Everything that happened to us is my fault. If we'd left when Noah wanted to, we would've escaped the storm. Easily. Instead, his bike is destroyed. Because of my recklessness. My stubbornness. If he hadn't insisted on leaving, would we still be there? Would we be battered by hail, cold, hurt, unconscious — or worse?

My tears fall hard and heavy. My parents were right. I'm too irresponsible. I'm a liability. And the people that suffer are the ones I love.

I can't do this. I have to end it with Noah before he gets hurt.

50

BREE

*R*ain falls on the roof of the loft and I groggily open my eyes. Usually, I'd be staring wide-eyed at the ceiling, excited and happy. But today, I'm filled with an aching sense of dread. Every drop crashes like the hail just days ago. I wince at the memory.

I squeeze my eyes shut against another day at Legacy. I've tried to stay positive but after what happened during the hailstorm, I can't. I can't risk hurting Noah and I'm too much of a coward to break up with him.

He needs to break up with me. And the best way to facilitate this is to show him who I am — not the helpful and supportive Bree he knows, but the worst parts of myself. I'm unreliable and irresponsible. I'll disappoint him eventually. So why does it hurt so much to see the pain in his eyes when I 'forget' to meet him or when I show up late?

Speaking of which... I check the time and see that I'm running late for work. Again.

I get out of bed and stretch. I've been sleeping terribly the past few nights and my audiobooks and scary movies can't even lull me to sleep. I picture a life far from Edendale to get to dreamland. In reality, escaping somewhere else might be my only chance to break free of the labels I've adopted.

Wild, irresponsible, careless Bree. Imagine if I could be anyone else.

I change into sweats and a hoodie and stroll to reception. Delia is sitting at my desk, speaking with a young woman and looking frazzled.

"Bree," Delia says. The young woman looks at me with exhausted frustration. "Ms. Hernandes booked herself into a two bedroom, but she's in a one bedroom. How'd that happen?"

"It's not a big deal," the young woman steps in. Her blue jeans and long sleeve shirt are lightly stained. "I have my toddlers with me and I was hoping for a good night's sleep, but it's fine."

She smiles, but I instantly feel bad for not paying more attention.

"What do you suggest we do?" Delia asks me, her tone patient and unaccusing. It breaks my heart to let her down, but it's inevitable. I'll only ever disappoint her too.

"Don't know." I shrug.

Delia stares at me for a long moment. I lower my gaze, I can't deal with her sparkling green eyes right now.

"Alright," Delia concedes, turning back to the computer. "Ms Hernandes, it appears that we do have an empty three bedroom suite. We'd be happy to upgrade you on the house. What do you say?"

Ms. Hernandes smiles radiantly. "That sounds perfect! Thank you."

Delia checks her in and insists that she'll help move her bags. Ms. Hernandes nods at me kindly and leaves reception. Delia, on the other hand, shoots me an exasperated look.

I sit at my desk and put on NWR. I'm both disappointed and relieved to hear that this bout of rainfall isn't accompanied by any severe weather — I'd love to catch a good storm, but the thought of going with Noah fills me with aching sadness.

I stare at the rooming list, but pay no attention. My phone pings and I open the text message, expecting it to be from Isla or someone from Edendale.

Nope. It's the dreaded Kate.

Hello Aubrey. It was lovely to hear from you a couple of days ago. Your dad and I were beginning to worry. Isla has been letting us know that you're well, but of course, we'd love to hear it from you.

I wanted to get in touch as Andrew Stewart is back from Saint Tropez. He's excited to meet with you for your coffee date at the end of the month. Please Aubrey, do be on your best behavior. We'll be back the next day and I cannot wait to hear about your progress. I'll send you a few suitable conversation topics in an email.

Love, Mom.

I throw my phone to the side and lay across the desk. I close my eyes while my exhausted mind copes with this. I never got around to telling my mom I won't be going on the date with Andrew Stewart.

I was too busy being happy.

51

NOAH

"Careful, amico! What are you doing?" Fernando moves my hand out of the way of the boiling water.

I snap to the present moment. "Sorry, I must've gotten distracted."

My mind was on Bree, yet again. Things are worse than ever and I'm analyzing everything that happened in the last couple of weeks for any clue. Sure, we hang out — when she shows up. I visit her at reception on my breaks, but she's cold and unwelcoming. And I haven't seen her in the kitchen since the hail storm.

"What were you thinking about?" Fernando takes the pot of water and places it on the counter.

"Nothing much." I run my fingers through my hair.

Fernando gives me a look. "It's Bree, isn't it?"

I take a deep breath and paste a neutral expression on my face. "Maybe we're not right together. It's never going to work between us."

"Why not?"

"She's a Lewis, I'm a Sawyer. She's too good for me. It's always going to be this way."

"Oh Noah," Fernando says, using my name for the first time in years. He places a firm hand on my shoulder. "How can my amichetto be so grown up and yet so stupid? You and Bree are meant to be. There's no way to fight that. Tell me, when did you first know that you loved her?"

I shrug. "I've always loved her."

"Exactly." Fernando slaps my shoulder. "Because you are meant to be."

I manage a laugh and roll my eyes. If only it was so simple.

"Get some fresh air." Fernando smiles. "Your shift is over and you need it."

I head to the reception, but when I get there, Bree is nowhere to be found. The portable radio is tuned into NWR. She'll be back soon.

I wander around the room. An unsettled feeling consumes me, trying to think of what I want to say. Since she mentioned Andrew Stewart in the meadow the other day, the question has been in the back of my mind like an annoying mosquito. Did she cancel the date?

A ping. The phone screen on the desk lights up.

It's Bree's phone.

Without meaning to look, I catch the subject line of an email.

Re: Your Date with Andrew

My blood goes cold and I'm hit with a pang of jealousy. That confirms it. She didn't cancel her date. Is that why she's been so distant — she wants to be with someone else? I have an overwhelming urge to see if there's any more information in the email, but that would be a massive violation of Bree's privacy.

Bree Lewis has a bright future and endless opportunities. She can do anything she wants, and be with whoever she wants. Me? I'm an amateur writer who works two jobs on top of my schoolwork to try and make ends meet for my family. It was silly of me to expect that we could be anything more than childhood friends.

I stare absentmindedly at the black phone screen, my mind racing. I take a breath but the action feels like knives in my chest. I'm just a fling, the middleman between "eligible Edendale bachelors." I'm the guy from the wrong side of the tracks, the perfect pawn to annoy her parents. How did I get it all so wrong?

"What're you doing here?" Bree's voice is cold when she walks into reception.

My heart stops. Did she catch me looking at her phone? Should I confront her and ask her about the email? But, how can I do that without her thinking I was snooping?

Instead, I say the first thing that comes to mind. "Meadow?"

My voice is a croak. As soon as the word is out of my mouth, I know that it's a bad idea. I won't be able to keep from asking her about the email, and she'll think that I don't trust her.

I open my mouth to backtrack and make an excuse, but Bree cuts me off, fixing me with a distant stare. "Sure."

I wander out of reception like a zombie, a pit of despair in my stomach. The logical part of me knows that I'm overreacting, it was just an email subject line. I've heard the way Bree speaks of Andrew Stewart — like a kid awaiting a piece of cold, overcooked broccoli.

But, in my heart, I understand why she's distancing

herself. She belongs with a worldly, rich guy like Andrew Stewart.

I walk into my cabin and grab a few things for the meadow. I open the top drawer of my dresser and pause, staring at the gift I got for Bree. It isn't much, it isn't glamorous by any stretch of the imagination, but I thought she'd like it. I've been thinking about it since the start of summer — a silly road trip guide.

I debate bringing the booklet with me. If she's distancing herself, should I bother giving her a gift? Would she even like something like this? Logic wins out. I bought it for her and I should give it to her, regardless of where I stand. I tuck the booklet into my back pocket before walking to Garth.

When Bree finally arrives, twenty minutes later, I'm sitting on the hood staring at Legacy Lake. Her expression is morose. I force a smile and give her a wave.

She frowns. "What about the alternator or whatever?"

She feels so far away. I open the door for her. "I fixed it a couple of days ago."

Bree nods her thanks and we get on the road. The silence in the car is anything but comfortable. There's a tension, a sourness, that fills me with dread. Bree must feel it too because she starts talking almost immediately.

"I heard from my parents today." Her happy tone is false.

"How're they doing?"

"Good, good." She stares out the window and we fall into an awkward silence. "They're loving Portugal, as you can imagine."

"Sure."

"But Europe, in general, is amazing. I love it there. I could move there someday, for sure..."

As Bree goes on, my shoulders slump. The gift in my

back pocket burns a hole through my jeans. Would she care about a road trip guide if Europe is where she wants to go?

I run my fingers through my hair. Is talking about Europe her way of telling me I'm not like the Stewarts — that I'm not good enough for her?

52

BREE

*W*hat am I even talking about? My words tumble out without any semblance of fore-thought. I wish Noah would stop me. "Legacy Inn has been the best experience. I wanted to be in Lisbon so bad, but Legacy worked well too."

My desperation rises. Why isn't this coming out correctly? I'm trying to say that, while Europe and Lisbon sound nice, nothing can compare to my experience working at the Inn this summer. The Legacy family means a lot to me; Noah means a lot to me.

It's the classic lead-in to a break-up. I've seen it in movies and read about it in books. You tell them everything you love and appreciate about them, and then do the whole 'it's not you, it's me' thing.

In this case, though, it truly is me.

Noah's face gets darker.

Panic creeps through me. I need to do this well or I might lose him forever. Maybe we can't be together, but I don't want my days to be entirely empty of Noah Sawyer. "This isn't coming out right. I'm sorry."

"I think you've made your point," he responds frostily.

I stare out the window and tears sting my eyes. I know what I need to do when we get to the meadow. I don't have a choice. I need to break up with him. The problem is that I love him with all my heart.

I loved him when we had our late-night conversations when we were kids. I loved him when we built forts and when I cried about my parents. I even loved him when he started pulling away from me. My heart ached for him when his mom passed away.

The years that we spent apart were the hardest of my life. I got used to being an outsider, a floater. I steeled myself against any vulnerability and never let myself imagine a future because it had already been planned for me. My singular goal was to have anything *but* that future.

Because of Noah, I felt excited about a different future, a future with him. My heart shatters, but my mind is made up. For Noah's own good, I need to end this.

He stops the car, puts it into park, and I almost keel over from dread. He undoes his seatbelt stiffly and I undo mine. The air is loaded, cold, severely uncomfortable. I open the door to escape, scrambling to think of what to say to get my feelings across.

Noah turns towards the trees and walks without taking my hand. I run after him and the bushes scrape my bare skin. I burst through the trees and Noah is walking towards the cliffs. The wind picks up and I hug my arms around myself. The storm isn't far.

We sit under the cliff overhang — him at one end and me at the other. My stomach turns over and I think I might throw up. I don't know what to say. How do I start this conversation? My teeth clack together. Without a word, Noah takes off his jacket and hands it to me.

"Thank you," I whisper.

The rain falls and I wrap myself in his jacket. It smells like him. I want to cry even more.

He's glacial, staring ahead. He's mad and maybe that's for the best. He won't fight for me if he's mad.

A flash of lightning cuts across the sky and my heart cracks with it. This is it.

53

NOAH

I stare at the horizon while sadness eats at me. Despite the storm, it feels too quiet under the cliff overhang. Like some depressing movie, we've reached the final scene. Everything is clear now — Bree wants a different life than what I can give her. I can't fight something this big. It's good that she's found where she belongs, even if that isn't with me.

I know Bree — she probably thought that the meadow was the perfect place to break up with me. So, I'm waiting. What will be her parting blow? Will she make an excuse, or will she be honest?

I bite my lip and I shake my head. This is what I expected. We're from different worlds. Our shared pasts don't mean we need to share a future together. But, for every break-up I've sat through — every one that I've initiated — never has it felt so meaningless and wrong.

Goosebumps rise on my skin but I barely notice. Bree is warming up with my jacket. I'm happy to give her one final thing before we part ways. The road trip guide feels lame and inconsequential now.

Rain thunders around us and the lightning blares through the sky. I would prefer to be in the mess of the storm right now. In the moments of silence, the weight of the truth presses upon us. We both know why we're here and what will happen when we leave.

Maybe I should fight for her, I *want* to fight for her. But, what can I say that will make any sort of a difference? Repeating "I love you" doesn't seem enough.

Bree opens her mouth and I wait for the words, bracing myself. Then, her jaw snaps shut. I scramble to think of something to say, anything to keep her with me, but nothing comes to mind. We fall into a defeated silence and reality hits. We're over. We're done. We're broken up.

I blink against the pain, feeling hopeless, wordless. Soon, the storm moves on and the world is quiet, too. We haven't moved, still sitting across the overhang from one another like two statues.

Then, Bree utters the words that shatter my heart, her voice detached. "Take me home."

54

BREE

*T*he next day, I call in sick for work for the first time all summer. I can barely open my eyes to face the daylight, let alone a dozen guests at reception. Delia is understanding, but I think she knows that I don't have an ordinary cold.

I spend the day in bed, tossing and turning, moving in and out of sleep. The loft is eerily silent, I can't bear to play my audiobooks or scary movies. My heart is broken into a million tiny pieces. Losing Noah is unbearable, but it's the best thing I can do for him. I was being selfish thinking that I could be with him.

Like my mom said — he's a great kid, responsible and organized. He has a solid future ahead of him, a goal. But me? I'm messy and aimless and I have no idea what I want. If Noah is a lightning strike, I'm a tornado.

The next morning, I force myself out of bed and tumble down to reception, my eyes half open. I knock something off the desk and Delia pops her head out of her office.

She takes in my sad state and her expression is concerned. "Maybe it's best you take today off as well, dear."

"What?" I ask groggily.

She leans against the doorframe, fiddling with her ring. "I've been working you too hard lately and I've noticed some... oversights in your work. I want you to take today off. Maybe explore the grounds, or relax in the loft, or perhaps head back to Edendale."

She walks over and takes my hand. "Please, don't take this as a criticism, dear. You've done amazing work this summer. Think of this as a thank you from me."

She smiles warmly, but my heart sinks. I know what she's implying. I've made too many mistakes lately and she wants me to leave. Once again, my carelessness has disappointed someone close to me.

I enter the loft and drop to the floor. I let the tears flow, curling into a ball and crying quietly into my fist. Everything that can go wrong has gone wrong. Noah and I are over, I've been booted from the Legacy family, and Delia — the person I saw as my mentor — is done with me. It was silly of me to think I had a home here.

In a couple of days, I'll be back in Edendale with a family I can barely identify as my own. I'll have to start the charade all over again and I'm tired of this game. I don't *want* to be irresponsible, careless Bree anymore. I wish I could start over, I wish I could be anyone but myself.

Familiar words echo in the back of my mind. This time, the voice isn't my mom's, my dad's or Delia's. The words are Noah's, but the voice is my own.

"You don't have to let them define you. You don't have to let their wishes choose for you."

The tears calm and my breath turns into hiccups. I repeat the words in my head over and over like some magic spell.

55

NOAH

*I*t's been two days since Bree and I broke up. Therefore, it's been two days since I slept. I walk through the kitchen on auto-pilot, grabbing this food item and that condiment. Carrie and Fernando's voices are blurred and unclear, like radio static is interrupting their frequency.

"Amico." Fernando places a hand on my shoulder, his eyes kind and worried. "Why don't you call it a day?"

"But my shift isn't over," I slice a tomato and juice flies everywhere.

"Yes, it is." Carrie bustles over and unties my apron. "Fer and I can take it from here."

I drop the knife, which appears, at second glance, to be a potato peeler. I let Carrie take the apron off my head and place it on a hanger. Fernando passes me a cupcake and gives me a warm smile as I'm shoo-ed through the door.

I walk through the event room and, without thinking, I pop my head into reception, unsure whether I want to see her or not. But, no chance. Delia looks up from Bree's desk.

"Can I help you, dear?" She takes off her half-moon glasses.

"I'm okay." I turn to walk away.

"She misses you too."

I pretend I don't hear her.

I walk along the gravel pathway and the rain pummels my back. A couple of weeks ago, Bree and I would've been watching this storm together. I wish I could turn back time. In a few days, we'll start our Senior year and the hardest thing will be seeing her at school and knowing that I can't hug her or kiss her. We'll never chase storms together.

With a sigh, I open my cabin door. I take a seat at my desk and turn on the lamp. I stare at a blank sheet of paper, unable to get her out of my head. Since our breakup, I can't think of a single thing other than her, and that includes the ending of my novel. I miss her smile, her eyes, her wit, her kindness. I'm kicking myself for not fighting for her, for not saying anything. I should have said something.

Frustrated, I pick up my notebook and skim through. I rip out a couple of pages, crumple them, and throw them across the room. This is why I should never have broken from the recipe. There's a reason my lifetime motto has been to help others and to put them first.

Bree was my childhood friend, my best friend, and my first love. I can't imagine my future without her, but she's better than where I come from.

56

BREE

*A*t some point, I'm aware that the side of my body aches and I stand. I sit on the bed and stare blankly at the wall. The crush of emotions has subsided and I've hit rock bottom.

I contemplate my life with a detached curiosity. Old Bree would've been thankful for a day off. She would've laid in bed for hours, treasuring her free time and snacking on fruit roll-ups. But, Old Bree doesn't exist anymore. Sometime in the past three months, she disappeared.

Working with Delia, I understood what it meant to have someone count on me. Dancing in the kitchen, I understood what it meant to feel comfortable and free. And chasing storms with Noah... I felt at home.

In the past few days, I've pushed away Noah and disappointed Delia. I've ousted myself from Legacy Inn. Ironically, I've finally succeeded at doing the thing I most wanted at the start of the summer — I'm being sent home. And I couldn't be more miserable.

Delia suggested I go back to Edendale for the day, but the summer is over anyway and the guests leave tomorrow.

My stomach turns over. Tomorrow is also my 'date' with Andrew Stewart and my parents are back shortly after. I can't bear to think about what that means.

I turn my head and realize my back is sore. The afternoon sun is warm on my face. Did I have breakfast or lunch today? I don't remember, I don't feel hungry anyway.

The one thing I do feel is resignation. There's no use in me staying here. In Edendale, I can mope in our big, empty house for a couple of days and put together a story as to why I got kicked out of Legacy — something perfect to piss off my parents.

Yet, where the thought of such planning used to fill me with a morbid thrill, I feel only exhaustion. I don't want to lie and I don't want to anger them anymore. The only thing I've wanted, for as long as I can remember, is a home.

I reach under my bed and grab my suitcase. Numb, I throw in pieces of clothing tainted with happy memories. The sunflower dress that I wore on my first date with Noah, the black lace top I wore when he told me he loved me, the red skirt I was wearing when I decided to try at my job.

After this whirlwind summer, I know one thing for certain — after graduation, I want to spend a year chasing storms. What comes after that is for future Bree to figure out for herself.

I empty my drawers and stack everything in my suitcase. By the time I'm done, the light is fading. I'll leave first thing tomorrow. I owe Delia a proper goodbye first.

I check my puffy eyes and swollen nose in the antique mirror. I'm about to hobble down the stairs when I remember one last item. I make my way to reception and Delia is seated at my desk — the receptionist's desk.

"Hi Delia." My voice cracks from lack of use and too many emotions.

"Hello dear," she frowns. "What are you—"

"Here." I shove my favorite pink cowboy hat into her hands. I haven't done good enough work lately to warrant a reward.

Delia stares at the hat and then meets my eyes. "What's this for?"

"It doesn't belong to me. It's yours."

Delia tilts her head. "I gave that to you for your great work this summer."

"I don't deserve it." I don't break from her gaze this time. I have no energy left to fight or argue.

Irritatingly, Delia doesn't take the hat. She floats around the desk and stands in front of me. She raises her arm and I think she might finally take the hat, but instead, she presses firmly on my wrist until the hat is by my side.

"Hun, of course you deserve this." Her eyes are kind and motherly.

"Why? I can't do this." I don't intend to sound tearful, I don't intend to cry. But the tears are coming down my face and I can't stop them. Delia takes me in her arms and gives me a big hug, a real hug. The kind you'd get from an aunt or a best friend or a parent.

"Bree Lewis." She pulls back and meets my eyes. "You can do anything you want to do."

"You don't know that."

Delia grips my shoulders firmly. "I've seen what you can do this summer, my dear. You can accomplish anything you set your mind to in your life."

Delia's words wrap around me like a warm blanket. I want to believe her so badly.

"But," I take a deep breath, hating the tearful, pathetic note in my voice. Delia grabs a tissue from the desk and wipes my cheek. "Why did you give me the day off?"

Delia laughs boisterously. She's still holding my shoulders and the force of her laugh shakes me. "I gave you the day off because you deserve it! After being sick yesterday, I wanted you to take another day. Plus, your parents messaged me..."

My tiny smile immediately drops off my face.

Delia continues. "They told me about your 'meeting' tomorrow and encouraged me to let you 'rest' beforehand. I don't know what all that's about, but given that you never asked for the day off, I figured you wouldn't be attending."

I nod, flabbergasted that my parents would go out of their way to message Delia about my date with Andrew Stewart. I look down, feeling emotionally wrung-out. "Actually, I was hoping to leave early anyway. I'd like a couple of extra days to get ready for school and all that..."

My voice trails off and I finger the rim of the pink cowboy hat in my hands. Delia's silent for a long moment and I sneak a glance at her face. Instead of anger of disappointment, she has a kind and compassionate expression.

"Of course, my dear. Vin and I can man reception for the next couple of days. You do what's best for you. I hope you know that you're welcome here at any time. You're a part of the Legacy family, and you always will be. There is a place for you here."

I smile tearfully and Delia wipes my face with the tissue again. She knows I'm not going back because of school. I'm leaving because of the person I love most, the one I can't face. I hug her one last time and then clutch the pink hat to my chest like it's a life preserver. "Thank you, Delia."

"If you still have the antique mirror, you can leave it in the loft. One of the guest room mirrors broke so I'll have Vin replace it with that one. And, speaking of which..." Delia whips off her glasses again, full of her theatrics. "If you were ever to decide to be a maintenance person, for example, we are sorely lacking in that department. Preferably working with wood. We have a *lot* of wood pieces to restore and to fix in the guest rooms — not to mention in the event room."

For the first time all day, I let out a laugh. "You'll be the first to know."

57

BREE

*T*he sky is dark when I make the decision to leave my bed. I had another sleepless night, but I might as well get on the road early. I roll over and check my phone clock.

5:37am.

Perfect time to wake up. Not.

I place my feet on the ground and stretch before going to my now-empty dresser. I scrounge for a piece of paper in the drawers and jiggle the one drawer that's been stuck all summer. Frustrated, I give it a hard yank and, to my surprise, the drawer slides open.

I freeze. The drawer contains two items — a night light shaped like a lion, and a photo I know well. I pick up the photo and smooth out the edges. In the foreground, young me, Isla, Victoria, Grace and Noah are smiling and laughing, our noses sunburnt and our lips dyed various colors of popsicles. In the background, a smiling woman has her arms around us all, looking carefree and unbelievably happy.

My heart thumps in my chest. Noah's mom.

I stare at the photo for ages. I must've stowed this away years ago, before she got sick. It's a reminder of the happy summers we all spent together. Back before everything fell apart.

Tears prick my eyes. I can't leave Noah without saying goodbye, but I also can't face him. I grab a pen from my suitcase and turn the photo over. On the back, I write two simple sentences — words that will hopefully convey what I'm feeling.

I look around the loft one final time and tidy the room, making my bed and closing the dresser drawers. I pack the night light, then I steel myself and descend the loft stairs for the last time.

Outside, the sky is gradually turning dark blue as the sun approaches the horizon. I walk dejectedly to Garth with all of my bags. A chilly breeze flows over me and I wrap my jacket around myself. Fall is on its way.

After placing my bags in my SUV, I head to the cabins. Noah should be at work by now. I didn't say bye to anyone else from Edendale High but I'll see them at school next week anyway. I spot Noah's cabin on the far edge, the window dark.

I'm torn. Part of me wishes he was still there. That we could say a proper goodbye. And the other part of me is relieved that I don't have to disappoint him one more time. I can leave the photo and skip out.

I press my ear to the door, listening for footsteps or shuffling, but all I hear is silence. My heartbeat echoes in my ears and my fingers tingle as I raise my hand to knock. Old Bree would've done this — demanded a confrontation, initiated a blow-out. But, I'm not her anymore. Instead, I reach into my back pocket and grab the photo, the beloved photo. I crouch and slide it under the door.

I force myself to turn around and walk away from the cabins at a normal pace. I perk up my ears to hear whether he opens his door, but I'm not sure which would be worse — for him to run after me, or for silence to follow me the entire way back to Garth.

What if he isn't working? What if he's looking at the photo, right now? I imagine the expressions on his face when he turns it over and reads my note. Is it possible that he's seen it and he's deciding not to follow me?

I spot the staff lot. And then, Garth. I'm getting closer and closer.

I open the driver's side door and my ears are still perked, listening for footsteps that never come.

58

NOAH

I pull the cinnamon rolls out of the oven and close the door with a hefty bang. It's six in the morning, and I'm thoroughly exhausted. Whenever I close my eyes at night, I see her face. I've taken to sitting at my desk, trying to finish my novel in between fitful naps on a blank sheet of paper.

"Morning!" Delia dances into the kitchen.

"Mi bella! You're up early this morning?" Fernando stares at early-bird Delia with his eyebrows raised. Delia is usually a muted version of herself until eleven in the morning.

"Indeed." Delia pours herself a cup of coffee and chugs it gratefully. "Last day with the guests and we're a woman down. I want to start wrapping things up."

"A woman down?" My voice is quiet and uneven.

"Yes, dear." Delia turns to me and sympathy glows in her eyes. "Bree is leaving this morning. She had a meeting of some sort..."

I can't hear anything else Delia says. There's ringing in

my ears and the remnants of my broken heart splinter further. Bree is going to meet with Andrew Stewart after all. I shouldn't be surprised. This is the way it's supposed to be. I place the cinnamon rolls on the counter and move numbly through the kitchen.

"Noah?" There's a blurred voice just out of reach.

The voice keeps speaking, but I'm so wrapped up in my thoughts, I don't register the words.

My mind is filled with the questions that have kept me up all night. Did I make a mistake? Should I have fought harder for her? How can I fight for her when I have nothing to offer? I can't bear the thought of giving Bree less than she deserves. Wanting her back is a selfish desire on my part.

"Noah!" A stern voice cuts through the haze and I look up in surprise.

"Finally!" Fernando's voice is unmistakably upset. "I called your name at least five times."

"Sorry, Fer, just distracted." I spread icing on a cinnamon roll.

"I'll say. You're spreading mayonnaise on my good rolls!"

Fernando is right. I grabbed a jar of mayonnaise instead of icing. I hurriedly wipe off the mayonnaise and Fernando rolls his eyes. Fernando has never used a tone like this with me. He's upset and angry, and the kitchen is dead silent.

"Bree's leaving today." His eyes search my face. "What are you still doing here?"

"I'm working." My voice sounds far away. "I'm helping you."

"No," Fernando says shortly. "You're hiding behind your job. Isn't that what you do? Hide behind your work and your family and your lack of time? Don't you see how crazy you two are for each other?"

His words are a slap in the face. I open my mouth to state my usual excuse. "But, Bree—"

"Bree Lewis," Fernando interrupts, "is one of the finest, most intelligent people you'll ever meet. But Noah? So are you. You two are meant to be together. Don't let her slip away."

A life without Bree — I couldn't imagine anything more miserable. Fernando's right. My days without her have not only been devastating, they've also felt deeply wrong — on some basic molecular level I can't comprehend. But it's too late. "She's going to meet with Andrew Stewart."

Predictably, Fernando has a response for this too. "L'amore vince sempre! This isn't just an old, silly Italian expression, amico. Love can and will conquer all, including time and space. It's never too late!"

Fernando's words sink in and I'm frozen. Love conquers time. Bree and I met before I can remember and we were friends for my entire life. The three years we spent apart simply don't matter in the grand scheme of what she means to me. Is our future linked too?

I can't let her go without a fight. The realization falls over me like a weighted blanket. There is only one truth — love conquers all — and, even if Bree doesn't want to be with me, I need her to understand that I will always be here for her.

"Gotta go." I bolt out of the kitchen.

The door slams behind me and I hear "Finally!"

I bound up the stairs to the loft, but the room is empty. The bed is made, the dresser drawers are closed and her absurd pile of blankets and pillows has disappeared.

I dash down the stairs, my heart in my throat. Please, let her be in the parking lot.

I run outside and get to the staff lot as fast as I can. No

sign of a silver SUV. I look around wildly, but my stomach sinks. Garth is gone. Bree is gone.

My eyes hover over my Bonneville and I make my decision. I need to run to my cabin.

Then, I'm going after her.

59

NOAH

*M*y feet tap the gravel pathway. My lungs burn. I slam open the door to my cabin and rummage through the dresser. Finally, I find the road trip booklet stashed deep in a drawer. I'm about to run back out when I spot something on the floor near the door.

In my hurry, it had almost been swept into the corner and out of sight. The only reason I saw it was because it wasn't crumpled up like the pages I'd rejected. Curiosity getting the better of me, I approach it and realize it's a photo. I pick it up and my heart stops.

It's a photo of the five of us kids seated on a bench, Bree's arm intertwined with mine. In the background, Mom is smiling. I can almost hear the sound of her laughter. I remember that day. We spent all day in the lake and came out when my dad arrived at Legacy. He had a surprise for us — popsicles.

Bree and I fought over this photo years ago. At some point, we thought the photo was lost and we stopped looking for it. I run my fingers over the surface of the photo tenderly and almost fall to my knees. She found it.

My fingers brush something ridged on the back and I turn the photo over. In Bree's cursive writing, there are two sentences.

I loved you then. I hope you can forgive me.

My heart races and I trace the imprint of the pen marks. Forgive her for what? For following her dreams? For pursuing Andrew Stewart?

A whirlwind of confused thoughts battle through my mind and I almost feel sick. A new feeling courses through me — something I haven't let myself feel for a long time. I'm angry. I'm angry for what happened to Mom. I'm angry for the childhood that was stolen from me. I'm angry for the stroke of bad luck that plagued me and my family. I'm angry that Dad lost his business. And I'm angry with myself for letting Bree Lewis go without a fight.

I need to catch her. Now.

I tuck the photo into my back pocket alongside her gift before throwing on my leather jacket. I race out of the cabin, running with renewed vigor towards the staff lot. I jump on my Bonneville and throw the bike in gear, peeling noisily out of the lot. But I don't care, let them all hear.

The only thing I know to be true is that I need to catch Bree before it's too late.

60

BREE

The tires hit smooth pavement and a tear falls down my face. I reach into the backseat and find one lingering fruit roll-up. I tear open the packaging with my teeth and chew through the roll.

I drive towards the horizon and consider the long road ahead of me, both literally and metaphorically. With Noah, I felt grounded and safe in the best way possible. Now that he's gone, my entire world is upside down. While I don't want to leave the Inn, the sadness is nothing compared to what I feel about leaving Noah.

I just need to get back to Edendale. There, I can mope in private. I can cry and scream and hold a pity party for myself.

Sometime overnight, I made a decision. I'm starting fresh and working on being myself, for myself. I'll tell my parents the truth about what happened at Legacy and I'll face them honestly. If they choose to continue prioritizing their businesses, that's their choice. Instead of rebelling and striving to go against what they want, I'm going to plan a future according to what I want and what feels right for me.

I don't want to give my parents the power to dictate who I am anymore. Why can't I decide for myself? Why can't I break away from the labels that have been cast upon me — reckless, irresponsible, careless? Why do I have to be placed in a box, never to escape or grow?

The anger expands within me and I reach into the backseat again, fluttering my fingers around for another fruit roll-up.

Vroom!

An ear-splitting noise approaches in the lane behind and then whips out onto the road beside me. The motorcycle is traveling quickly in the wrong lane. Before I can register what's happening, the horn blares.

"What the?!"

I whirl around to look at the person on the bike, glaring with everything I have.

The visor flips up and it's Noah. He indicates for me to turn off onto the road ahead. With a lump in my throat, I lower my window and shriek at him to get back in the right lane.

Then, a truck appears in the distance, coming fast towards him. Adrenaline bursts through me. The truck isn't slowing down.

"Get back Noah, please get back!" I shout manically.

The truck blares his horn.

I slow down so Noah can tuck in ahead of me just in time.

The driver gives me a furious scowl as he drives by.

I'm shaking. That was way too close.

I turn onto the gravel road and follow the line of dust protruding from Noah's motorcycle. I feel nauseous and my tears are now of anger and not sadness. Why was he driving in the wrong lane? Did he want to get hurt? Did he want to get killed?

Finally, he pulls off. The blood pumps fast in my veins.

"What were you thinking?" I yell as I slam the driver's side door. "Were you *trying* to get killed?"

Noah takes off his helmet and places it firmly on the bar that used to hold the side-view mirror. He stalks over to me and I realize that his face is dark and his brows are furrowed. He's angry too. Old Bree would have felt a thrill. She would have been morbidly proud that she got a rise out of him. But, New Bree just feels angrier.

As if on cue, a rumble of thunder booms and that's when I finally look around. I recognize that field and those trees. Ahead, the peaks on the horizon are grey instead of white — but they'll be snow-covered again soon. We're parked in our spot by the meadow. In the distance, the sky is as angry as I am. Blue and purple clouds hover ominously.

It's coming our way. But for once, I barely pay attention. I'm too upset with Noah, and with my parents, and with my life. He stands in front of me, his shaggy hair hanging over his eyes.

"Want to tell me about this?" He holds out the photo, his voice low. "You hope I can forgive you? Forgive you for what?"

My breath catches. I scramble for a response. Best to resort to what I'm angry about.

"You do realize you almost killed us both?" The thunder booms again in the distance, fueling my rant. "I've never seen anything so irresponsible, so reckless, in all my life. Don't you see how dangerous that was? What were you thinking..."

My words are a speech that's already been written.

They're the same words I've heard from my mom my entire life. A drop of horror crawls down my spine as I realize that I'm saying these things because I care about Noah. I love him.

But then, what does that say about my mom?

By the time I've exhausted my monologue, Noah is no longer looking angry or upset. In fact, he has a tiny smile on his face.

"WHAT are you smiling about?" I finish, more exasperated than ever.

Noah shrugs and his eyes twinkle. The first drop of rain hits his cheek. "I got a rise out of you."

He's smiling his trademark half-smile, and the rain is falling harder now. His blue eyes are traveling over my face, like he's trying to memorize me.

My heart starts to give in and that's when I panic. No. Bree. No.

I wrote that so he'd *understand*, not so he'd chase me down and make me doubt everything I had felt so sure about. My resolve threatens to melt away and my walls almost break, but I take a deep breath and do the hardest thing I've ever had to do. I steel myself against every single emotion he brings out in me.

I know what I need to say. It's the only thing I can do to protect him.

61

NOAH

*H*ow does Bree have this power over me? I'm smiling, even though she just yelled at me for being careless. I'm vaguely aware that the rain is falling in inconsistent droplets. Even though she's angry and I'm upset, I have to acknowledge that I missed her. I miss her still.

I hold out the photo. Ironic, for the writer to be lost for words when it counts the most. I want to tell her how much she means to me, but how can anyone put that into words when the entire planet, galaxy, universe, isn't enough?

"I love you, Bree. I always have," I say quietly, "you're everything to me."

"Noah, don't you get it?" She interrupts, her voice angry. "I'm only ever going to hurt you. You need to stay away from me."

My eyebrows shoot up in surprise. I tilt my head to the side. "You really think that?"

Bree's chest rises and falls and she appears to be out of breath, but she doesn't drop my gaze. She nods and crosses her arms coldly.

She thinks she's going to hurt me? All of a sudden, her loaded questions and distance makes sense. My eyes are pleading as I look at her face, but her decision has been made. I hold the photo awkwardly. The gift is tucked underneath, but I can't bear to tell her about it.

"I guess I'll see you at school then," I say, handing her the photo with the road trip booklet. She takes it absent-mindedly. I salute her and go back to my bike.

With every step, my brows draw in further. I need to say my part before I let her go. Before she meets with Andrew. "I thought we had something special. I understand why you're doing this and why you're choosing him. You're the most incredible person I've ever known and I love you for every bit of your wild side. To me, you were always just Bree. Like a firecracker, ball lightning, the love of my life."

I place the helmet on my head, refusing to meet her eye. "Good luck on your date with Andrew. The Stewart family... seem great. If you want to be friends, I'll be your friend forever. And even though I'm not enough, I promise I'll try to be your home, always."

*N*oah's words shock me to life. They're the words my heart aches to hear. But I can't let my resolve weaken, I can't risk hurting him. I run my fingers absent-mindedly over the photo. That's when I realize that Noah gave me more than just the photo. I feel metallic rings and a plastic backing. I lift the photo and find a small booklet.

Road Trip Guide to the Best Storm-Watching Locations in North America

Goosebumps flutter over my skin and I realize what Noah has been saying to me all along. He'll *always* be my home. I can be who I am — wild and free, or reliable and consistent — and Noah will be there for me just the same. Supporting me, no matter what. He'll be my home base, my stable ground.

A warm feeling of calm flows through me. Even though the rain is approaching, the lightning is minutes away, and the wind is picking up, the world has never felt so beautiful.

Noah puts a leg over his motorcycle, ready to get into gear.

"I was never going to meet Andrew." My words have the

desired effect. Noah pauses. "I texted my mom to let her know that I wouldn't be meeting him. Delia let me go early because I said I wanted a few days to collect myself before school. But the truth is, I couldn't stand to lose you."

The sky breaks open and a steady rain falls. I tuck the photo and the booklet into my jacket. Noah's frozen on his bike and I can't see his face for the visor.

"There's just one person I want to spend my time with." I slowly walk towards him, like I'm approaching a wild animal. "I'm crazy about you Noah. I'm yours and I was always yours. It was never a question."

I'm getting closer now and my heart is racing. I reach out and place my hand on top of his. "My life is a mess and I don't know what I want for my future. People say I'm unreliable and careless and irresponsible, but I want to be better. You make me want to be better, even though it scares the life out of me. I want to travel and road trip and chase storms with you. I want my future to include you. My future is you."

I'm in front of him now, and he turns to face me. He lifts his visor so I can see his face. His blue eyes search for mine and I finally understand what people mean by love conquers all. I'd conquer anything for him.

"You sure?" His voice is low and I meet his gaze with my own level stare.

"Never been more sure of anything in my life."

He lifts the helmet from his head and I put my arms around him. In his eyes, I can see, so clearly, our future together, our past together, and our present together. He gives me his trademark smile and my legs go numb. Thankfully, he pulls me close, wrapping an arm around my waist. He grazes his fingertips along my cheek and I run my fingers through his hair.

Then, above our heads, a massive ray of light.

We look up in tandem and see one of the world's rarest phenomena — ball lightning.

I'm breathless, watching the ball of light fly through the sky and away from us. It occurs to me that the things I once found so rare — so incomprehensible — are actually possible.

I turn towards him, speechless, and get lost in his intense blue-eyed stare — the one I want to see every day, forever. I run my eyes over his face, wanting to memorize every moment, every tiny detail.

When his lips meet mine, I know that it isn't just a kiss. We're living our future and I can't wait a moment longer.

63

BREE

"So... Power of immortality or psychic abilities?" I bite into a fruit roll-up.

"If I had psychic abilities, I might be able to predict when you're going to snag the next fruit roll-up." Noah looks at me pointedly and I blow him a kiss.

Noah and I are making dinner for his family in his kitchen. The house hasn't changed one bit since I was a kid. The living room is still tidy, but messy enough to be homey. The kitchen is stacked high with various dishes and cookware. The hallways are filled with candid shots of the entire family, including a section with photos of his mom. We added the photo I found at the Inn to the collection.

I jump off the kitchen counter and wrap my arms around him. "What can I do?"

"Oh, *now* you want to help?" He laughs, chopping tomatoes.

"Don't you get it? That's my specialty." I pick up a slice of tomato. "I come in at the last minute and change everything."

He looks at me, a twinkle in his eye. "As raccoons do."

He gestures to the cutting board next to his, piled high with peppers and lettuce. A song comes on the radio and Noah and I dance before continuing to chop vegetables. The pans of veggies are sizzling and the water is boiling. Upstairs, Victoria and Grace are screeching about one thing or another. The house is loud and full of happy noises.

"Smells good in here!"

A familiar booming voice echoes through the kitchen and I whirl around. Noah's dad looks the same as ever, but with slightly thinner hair and a dapper mustache. He's wearing work slacks and his shirt is tucked in.

"What're you doing home?" Noah exclaims and his dad walks over to give him a big hug.

"I asked for the night off! I couldn't miss my son's first night back after three months." He pats Noah on the back before turning to me. "This can't be... Bree Lewis?"

"In the flesh." I say with a beaming smile to match his.

"My goodness... you've grown!"

"You must be the only person in the world who thinks that." I laugh and he bends over to give me a hug.

Noah's dad is as kind and charismatic as I remember. His smile is unbelievably contagious and I can see where Noah gets his quick wit and sincerity. We catch up for a few minutes before he goes to change. I return to my tomatoes with a smile still on my face.

"What're you smiling about?" Noah asks with a laugh in his voice.

"Nothing," I say, and then, "everything."

Noah gives me a kiss on the cheek and I set the table. In truth, I'm incredibly, indescribably, overwhelmingly happy right now. This house — this home — is exactly what I've been looking for my entire life. But, in truth, I had it all along. Home can be found in many places.

I'm excited for the year ahead, or many years, spent with Noah. A plan for myself is starting to form and I can't wait to get started. This year, my Senior year, I'm going to try in all of my classes. I'll get a part-time job to make some money so that I can spend the year after graduation road tripping across America. Noah wants to come with me, we've already talked about it. He wants to write on the road, assuming his family can make do without him.

Eventually, we'll come back to Edendale and maybe I'll work at Legacy Inn. Maybe, someday, I'll run it. Legacy is my home and the Legacy family is my own. If Delia can run the Inn — with her so-called wild and untameable character — so can I.

64

NOAH

"Vic, Grace! Dinner!" Bree hollers up the staircase as I put the final dish on the table. We're having a Fernando classic tonight — cheeseburger tacos. The two hooligans come crashing down the stairs, followed quickly by Dad. He looks well, if not slightly stressed.

I take a breath and push my worries to the back of my mind to enjoy dinner with my family. It's our first night back in Edendale and Bree is over for dinner. I smile listening to the happy conversations happening all around me. Just like when Mom was here.

"So, Bree, what're your plans post-graduation?" Dad asks and then takes a bite of taco.

"I want to go on a road trip across America."

"Phenomenal idea. It's a great way to get to know the country. Will Noah be going with you?"

Dad glances at me and I offer a feeble smile. The truth is, I'd love to go, but I'm not sure I can do it. I can't leave them — Dad and my sisters need the income. I want to go with her, to travel across America with her, but it feels like a pipe dream.

"I'm not sure it'll work out." I say and Bree squeezes my hand under the table. We both want this, but we know that my family has to come first.

"Why not?" Dad asks, frowning.

"I want to be here for you guys. Help with money and all that."

Dad drops his taco and shakes a finger at me. "You've done more than your share over the years, kid. I can't tell you how much I appreciate that you jumped in to help us after your mom died."

Everyone at the table is still and you could hear a pin drop. Dad never talks about Mom's death.

He takes a deep breath and goes on. "We're back on our feet now and it's time for you to be a kid, to enjoy yourself and your life. I've leaned too hard on you in recent years, and I'm sorry for that. Go. We'll be just fine here."

Bree squeezes my hand again but I feel frozen. A weight lifts from my chest, threatening to send me floating off into space. I grip her hand harder, hoping she can hold me down.

"I feel like you're a little *too* anxious to get me out of the house." I joke and the tension is broken.

Dad rolls his eyes and laughs, gesturing to the twins. "Besides, these two have good news on that front."

Grace drops her fork with a clatter and looks at me excitedly. "The shop wants to extend my contract into the year. They're totally fine with me working part-time while I'm in school. Apparently, their *top designer* will be in town and I might get the chance to work with her. Imagine — me working with a *designer!*"

Grace's squeals are followed by Victoria's quiet announcement, a glint of excitement in her eyes. "And the library asked me if I wanted to do some archival work for them on the weekends. It's the best experience I could ask for to get into a top pre-law program!"

I sit back and enjoy the laughter while everyone speaks about what the next year holds for them. I meet Dad's eyes and his nods at me, raising his glass.

"So, Dad," Grace adds a piece of cilantro to her taco with a flourish. "Any luck with the job?"

Dad's face falls and my heart falls with it. Not a good sign.

"They still aren't looking to hire anyone full-time."

"None of the contracts worked out?" I ask, my voice quiet.

Dad was working for a few different companies in town over the summer. We were all hoping one of the contracts would be extended, or he'd be offered a permanent position. But, he shakes his head sadly. I stare at my food. At least the option is there for me to return to Colman's and Spruce Tree.

"Have you tried Legacy?" Bree pipes up quietly and the table goes silent again.

"What do you mean?" I ask, my brow furrowed.

"Delia was speaking to me the other day." Bree shrugs. "She said they have a *lot* of maintenance projects on the go right now. There's a ton of work to do with wood furniture in the guest rooms and the event room. I'm sure she'd be more than happy to have a carpenter on board, given that Vin is so busy."

I nod slowly and a glimmer of hope comes alive. Someone to help Vin with maintenance? Delia can't say no to that.

"What do you think, Dad?" I ask, looking over at him.

He has a tentative smile on his face, cautiously considering. "It's an intriguing option. I always loved Legacy and I was so happy when your mom got a job there. I haven't been there in years." He glances at the twins before going on. "I can't stay there permanently, but I can bring some of the furniture here to work on it in the workroom."

I look at Bree and she's smiling shyly. If it's possible, I think I love her even more.

Dad gives Bree a grateful nod. "It's a wonderful idea, Bree. I'll give Delia a call first thing tomorrow."

Bree nods and blushes. She meets my eyes and my heart swells with joy.

65

BREE

*W*hen I get to my house, my face hurts from smiling. For the first time in a long time, I feel excited and calm as I close the front door. No matter where life takes me, Noah has shown me something so valuable. Home can be whatever I want it to be. Home is Legacy, Noah, Isla, Delia, Fernando and Carrie. Home is Garth when I speed towards a storm.

And right now, my house is not my home. But I want it to be.

To my surprise, there's a light on, way down the hallway in our family room. Did I leave a light on by mistake all summer?

Confused, I drop my bag and wander towards the light. Goosebumps rise on my skin. Vampires? Aliens? Ghosts? Please, don't let it be a ghost. Or a raccoon.

My heart is racing when I reach the doorway. Slowly, I peer into the family room.

And there are my parents, sitting on the couch. My mom is reading a magazine and my dad is passed out. What are they doing here? Aren't they supposed to be in Europe?

"Hi," I say awkwardly and step into the light.

"Hello, Aubrey." My mom drops her magazine, her voice tired but not unkind.

"You're back?"

"We changed our flight." She stands up and elbows my dad. His head lolls and she rolls her eyes, giving up on him. "You canceled the date with Andrew Stewart."

I take a breath and remind myself why I'm here, how this summer changed me. Old Bree would have flown into a sarcastic word war, but I don't want to put up the front anymore. It's exhausting.

"Yes, I did," my voice is calm and level, no longer biting. "I don't want to date Andrew Stewart. In fact, I don't want to date any of these guys you set me up with."

She picks up her phone and a flash of pain travels through me. I forgot about this — her inability to keep attention for one conversation.

"You know that's rude, right?" My voice isn't angry or upset, it's like hers — tired and sad. She looks at me in confusion. "Texting. While we're having a conversation. You do it all the time."

Her eyebrows shoot up and she places her phone to the side.

I breathe a small sigh of relief. I would've preferred to have the full day tomorrow to rehearse what I want to say. But, after tonight's dinner with Noah's happy family, my feelings are fresh and raw. It's a small improvisation to express feelings I've had for a long time. "Kate, sit down. I have some things to tell you."

And for the first time, I have a real, adult conversation with my mother. In our family room where she 'ruined' my summer months ago, I express everything I've felt for years — the pain and anger and sadness. I tell her how much it hurts to be called 'reckless' and 'irresponsible'. And I tell her that love isn't overrated, because I've found love with Noah.

It feels like hours have gone by when I reach the end of my speech. It was surprisingly eloquent for not being practiced, but my words were genuine. To my utter surprise, my mom doesn't glance at her phone once. She doesn't open her mouth or argue. She listens.

"Aubrey," she finally whispers and something deep stirs in my soul. "I'm... I'm so sorry."

She drops her head and stares down at her hands. I have no clue what to do. I'm picking at my fingernails. This is a highly unusual interaction for us.

"I didn't intend..." She starts, and then tries again. "I didn't mean..."

She sighs deeply and then looks at me. For the first time, I see my mother as a person. She's no longer my overbearing, bullying mom. She's just a woman, confused and uncertain herself. "I respect you for bringing this to me. I know you've felt this way for a long time. There was always a gap between us, something separating us. I didn't know how to fix it, and apparently I made it worse."

I blink.

She continues. "I'm sorry for making you feel this way. I guess I only ever saw you one way and never spent time getting to know every side of who you are. With the Inns and everything, I forgot what truly mattered. It's not an excuse, by any means."

Her eyes are turquoise, like mine, but hers are lined with soft makeup. They glisten.

"Your words strike home on several levels," she says quietly. "The truth is, those are the very words my mother used to describe me."

What?!

"Bree, I was very much like you and my mom used to say the same things to me. I must've internalized her words and then made you feel the same way I used to feel."

This is too much. My mom was 'wild' like me?

"Really?" I croak, my throat dry. "You?"

"The things I used to get myself into..." My mom has a half-smile and she seems lost in some distant memory. All of a sudden, she looks really young. "Did you know I took Delia for her first skydive? She became obsessed with it. Though of course, I had to stop..."

She glances at my dad and a flash of sadness crosses her face. Wait a minute. Was my dad her Andrew Stewart?

"I wouldn't blame you if you could never forgive me." She reaches for my hands. "But I would love to get to know the real you, the real Bree. What do you think?"

Her words cover me like warm water and my shoulders relax down my back. Is this real? Is any of this happening right now? Years of anxiety, anger and grief have piled up so high within me that I'm not sure I can ever tear my walls down for her. But I want to try.

"We'll see. Mom."

I offer her the smallest smile, but perhaps the first genuine smile I've given her in years. Her palms are warm around mine and she smiles wide. For the first time ever, I feel like my mom is seeing me.

Spontaneously, I lean forward and wrap my arms around her. I give her the hug I always wanted to receive from her, and she wraps her arms around me in response. We stay there for a long while, clasped around each other, and I finally start feeling at home.

66

BREE

"That was a pretty hefty conversation you had with Mom and Dad this morning." Isla takes her lip chap out of her bag before lowering the air conditioning. Garth is suddenly filled with the scent of blue raspberry.

I sigh and tug on the elastic on my wrist. "Hefty, but necessary."

"At least you told them. Finally." She giggles and then bolts out of the car, off to school.

"Have a great day, La." I say and she slams the door shut. Through the open window, I say, "You know I'm always here for you right?"

Isla gives me a wink. "Ditto."

She heads towards school, ready to start the next semester with a bang. I smile and watch her go. I can't believe how much my little sister has grown over the summer. She's tanned and her hair is blonder than ever. Her backpack is almost the size of her, ready for her textbooks.

I hum under my breath and circle around the school looking for parking. My mind immediately travels back to this morning's conversation, when I finally told my parents I wanted to take a year off for storm chasing. Things with my mom have slowly been improving, but the news was a hard pill for her to swallow.

Still, I can tell that she's working on our relationship as hard as I am. Delia calling to rave on and on about my good work at Legacy over the summer only seemed to sweeten matters further. Mom even gave me a tentative hug afterwards.

By the time I'm at my locker and stacking my textbooks, I have an absurdly bright smile for the first day of school. Noah's coming to meet me soon so we can walk to our first class together. Even though we've spent every day together over the last three months, I'm most excited to see his face when I wake up in the morning.

I shut my locker door and glance around the hallway. Isabella Hall and Lucas Therborn storm past me and I roll my eyes. There's always drama with Isabella. I spot Kiara and Jonathan walking with a couple of friends and Kiara smiles at me.

"Hey, Lewis."

There's that familiar husky voice. I turn around to find Noah leaning against the lockers, wearing his leather jacket and smiling his beautiful half-smile. He's holding a fruit roll-up in his hand.

"That for me?"

"How else could I bribe you to walk the halls with me on the first day of school?"

"Good thinking. It's tough to be seen with the likes of you." I open the package and take a bite as Noah kisses me on the cheek.

I wrap my arm around his waist and we walk down the hallway, garnering a few stares. I guess people weren't expecting Noah 'the mysterious hottie' and Bree 'the wild child' to get together. Along the way, I spot Anaya talking to someone in the gym. I wonder how her summer turned out.

"Did your dad hear back yet?" I ask mid-bite.

Noah smiles widely. "Delia called last night. He got the job."

I squeal in delight. Delia did it! The Inn had to move a few things around for budgeting, but she seemed excited to have Noah's dad on board. And now, he has a permanent, full-time position with Legacy Inn.

"So... next year..." I trail off, hoping against hope for good news.

"I *guess* we can take a road trip together," Noah says with a teasing smile.

"Yes!" I exclaim and kiss him on the cheek.

Then, Noah pauses in the hallway and reaches into his bag. "I want to show you something."

With a flourish, he produces his well-worn notebook. My heart jumps into my throat as I flip through the pages. "You finished it?"

Noah's eyes are sparkling and he nods. "I brought it to a publisher a couple of days ago and he loved it. He wants to see the finished novel, typed and ready to go, in the next couple of months."

He points to the bottom of the last page. "Your note inspired me."

I read the last sentence aloud, "I loved you then. And I always will."

My heart might explode in my chest and my stomach is filled with butterflies. I meet his gaze and my smile matches his.

"Check the front," he says and I immediately flip through to the front of the book. It's an Acknowledgements page with just two names on it.

"Nina Sawyer"

"Bree Lewis"

I'm officially speechless. Tears spring to my eyes but these are tears of pure joy. I cradle the notebook in my hands, not ready to let it go.

"Without you," Noah says quietly. "I couldn't have written this novel, couldn't have pictured my future. I love you and I will always love you. I'll follow you across the world if that's where you want to go."

My face breaks into a beaming smile. I stand on my tip-toes and give him a proper kiss, the world singing around us.

As Noah and I approach our first class of the day, I'm overwhelmed by how grateful I am for this life-changing summer. Three months ago, I was lost and unsure of my future. Since then, I found out who I am and I learned to be proud of it. I'm excited about a life unaffected by the expectations of people around me. And I had my world turned right-side up by a boy I've known forever.

Finally, I'm home.

Thank you for reading!

If you enjoyed the story, I'd appreciate if you were able to leave a review! As a new author, reviews mean everything to me, and I'm so grateful for each and every one of them.